Always Remember

Denise Judge

Always Remember

ISBN-10: 0986115304

ISBN-13: 978-0-9861153-0-1

First Edition: February 2015

Cover Design by Ann McMan

This trade paperback original is published by
Blithe Press, Richmond, VA.
www.Blithepress.com

ACKNOWLEDGMENTS

Many years of my life have gone into the process of completing this, my first published work. I am eternally grateful to Golden Crown Literary Society (GCLS) for sponsoring the mentor/mentee program. I am beyond blessed to have been accepted and assigned to work with the amazing Susan X. Meagher. Without Susan's input and encouragement I am not convinced I would ever have completed this book. Thank you for your invaluable input, suggestions and encouragement.

No work is complete without a great editor. I am fortunate to work with the amazing Heather Flournoy. Thank you for your input, suggestions and always keeping my point of view intact.

I fell in love with the first cover draft Ann McMan sent. Thank you Ann for being so easy to work with and for sharing your talent. Without reading a single word, you captured the essence of this book with the cover you designed.

It was terrifying to send the first draft to other's to read. With great angst, I made that move and placed my trust in beta readers Ci-Ci Thomson and Ellen Elhard. Thanks ladies. You are the best.

A special thank you to Lori L. Lake for sharing your wealth of knowledge, your encouragement and just being a great lady.

If you are reading this, I hope you enjoy my story. I thank you for spending your time and money and taking a chance on me.

Last, but certainly not least, thank you to Wende for understanding how much this means to me. How boring my life would be without you.

If you love something, set it free. If it comes back to you, it's yours. If it doesn't, it never was.

~Chinese Proverb

CHAPTER 1

Raynee Waters sat in the warm sand burrowing her feet into the softness. Looking out over the deep blue of the Atlantic Ocean, her mind was a thousand miles away. This place was so much like home to her, yet she felt cold and alone. She didn't know how long she had been sitting there, when she realized there was a sailboat in the distance. A small smile broke across her face. Jumping up, she jogged toward the house.

Picking up her cell phone, she dialed the familiar number. "Hi." she said when Sam answered.

"Hi yourself," he replied. "What's up?"

"Not much, I'm at the beach house. I thought you might want to come down tomorrow." she said with an obvious lack of enthusiasm.

"Are you okay? Do you need anything?" Sam asked with concern.

"No, I don't need anything except to see you."

"See you in the morning," Sam said before hanging up.

◊◊◊

Raynee was lying in the bed when she heard Sam's car door slam. She hadn't slept again last night and wondered if she would ever sleep again. She jumped up and threw on her favorite T-shirt and shorts. She ran to the door, yanked it opened and grabbed him as he was turning the key in the lock. She laughed when he almost lost his footing from the quick movement of the door.

"Hi, good looking,"

Dropping his bag, he scooped her up, once again showing her he was no longer the little brother whose diapers she had once changed. Placing her back on the floor, he gave her a soft hug.

"Hi ya sis." he replied as he looked lovingly into her eyes.

He was the best little brother a girl could ask for. Sam was tall and thin, with straight dark brown hair and dark brown eyes--Cow eyes, his first grade teacher had once said. His friends still teased him about it. To her they were the eyes she knew she could look into when she laughed and when she cried.

"I'll bet you're beat. Drop your bag in your room and come into the kitchen. I'll get us something to drink.

◊◊◊

Sam sat at the kitchen bar while Raynee put the ice in the glasses and poured both of them a diet soda. He watched his sister's movements and listened to her short answers about her week alone at the beach house. The lack of sleep shone on her face like an unwanted guest. Sam knew something was wrong when he had received the phone call. He and Raynee weren't just siblings; they were close friends. Sometimes he felt like Raynee shouldered the burden of a parent when it came to him. She was a caring, compassionate person, but she could also be very closed when it came to her own feelings. Sometimes it wasn't what she said, but rather what she hadn't said, and today, it was what she still wasn't saying.

Raynee placed the drinks on the bar and sat on the stool beside Sam. "So, how's school going?"

"Not bad, but I'll be glad when this semester is over. I'm ready for a break."

"Are you keeping your grades up?"

"Yes ma'am." He laughed at Raynee's concern. Sam was an A student and Raynee knew it, but she always checked in on him.

"How's Lexie? Are things going okay with the two of you?"

"She's doing well. With our school schedules we don't see each other very often."

"Well, tell her hello for me when you see her."

"Will do."

"It's going to be a beautiful day, let's sit outside." Reaching out, she took Sam's hand as she slid off the barstool.

Hand-in-hand they walked onto the deck and sat in the warm morning sun. Late summer was the best time to go to the beach. The summer crowds were gone and the snowbirds had not yet arrived.   Looking across at his sister, Sam asked how things were going. Raynee gave him that look, the one that said, "Not yet." "So when did you come down?" Sam inquired, trying to get her to talk.

"Sunday," she replied. It was now Thursday and Sam wondered what was going on for his sister to be here alone and not call him for three days. "I just needed a little break and things were slow at Pabulum. Chandler and Alex are coming down tomorrow. You will stay won't you? They would love to see you."

"Absolutely, I haven't seen them in ages," he said. He knew the three of them could put that beautiful smile back onto his sister's face. "Besides, do you think I would turn down an opportunity to get one of your fantastic meals?" Then with a slight look of fear in his eyes added, "You are cooking aren't you?"

Raynee laughed. She obviously suspected her brother ate junk food most of the time. Having a chef for a sister did have its perks.

"I think I'll put on my suit and take a walk on the beach. Care to join me?" Raynee inquired, the sadness back on her face.

"No, you go ahead. I think I'll do some studying. Just because I skipped class today doesn't mean I can skip studying too."

"You will be one hell of a lawyer someday...if you'll stop letting people like me keep you from your classes," Raynee said in what was clearly an attempt to lighten her mood. Then she was up and in the house before Sam could reply.

◊◊◊

Staring into the mirror, Raynee ran her hands through the wavy length of hair. *I have to do something with this*, she thought. Pulling it back into a ponytail, she caught her eyes in the mirror. Her distinct eyes elicited lots of comments from those who happened to notice one was green and the other brown. She found it amusing that people who had known her for years would stop in mid-conversation and give her a funny look. She always knew what was coming next. With a puzzled look on their face they would ask, "Are your eyes different colors?" She laughed and smiled at the question. She liked that her eyes were different. Today she thought they looked like Christmas with all of the red streaks in them. She had to get some sleep. *Maybe with Sam here, I can sleep tonight.*

She pulled on the black and silver two-piece suit. *At least I have a good tan.* Although, she did not need to lose more weight, her 5'6" frame looked too thin. Payton liked her body, she remembered. She had to stop it, stop thinking of Payton. She should be thinking of....maybe she shouldn't think at all.

Jogging down the beach, the wind whipping through her hair, Raynee felt better. If she just didn't think about "it." She would rather just escape for now...just enjoy the beach, the sun and spending time with Sam, Chandler, and Alex.

◊◊◊

Raynee had met Chandler McCord while she was in culinary school. It had only taken them a few days to realize they had a lot in common. The two ladies had developed a deep bond and twelve years later they were still best friends. After culinary school, Chandler opened a catering business. She now supplied desserts for Pabulum, the restaurant Raynee co-owned. Six years ago, Chandler met Alex Richardson and the two had become inseparable. They were a perfect match and a strikingly beautiful couple. Both tall and lean, Chandler had short thick brown hair, bright green eyes and a killer smile. By contrast, Alex had long blonde hair with deep blue eyes. Whenever they were out together, they were ogled by both sexes. They both loved the attention and would often play it up by cooing at each other. They enjoyed food, golf, and traveling, but mostly they just enjoyed being together. Raynee, too, had grown to love this woman who made her friend so happy.

Raynee laughed at the sudden growl coming from the pit of her stomach. She hadn't had much of an appetite for the last several months, not since she had starting receiving the phone calls.

Maybe she could talk Chandler into making a cheesecake. Raynee had a huge weakness for Chandler's cheesecake. That would help her to put some weight back on. Payton had loved cheesecake as much as Raynee did. She remembered the time... She was doing it again. Did she have any memories that didn't include Payton? Raynee fell into the soft sand dune and dropped her face into her hands. The salty tears rolled down her face while the salt water lapped at her toes. She didn't know how long she had been sitting there lost in thought, but when she lifted her head Sam was walking towards her, his hands stuffed into his pockets. He had such a carefree walk. She wished she had his outlook on life right now. Although she knew things would get better, right now she wasn't sure when that would be.

Sam reached down to pull his sister to her feet. Holding her to his chest, he placed a soft kiss on top of her head.

She looked up into his face and said, "Okay, I guess I should explain a few things to you".

"Not unless you're ready, sis." he replied as they began walking back to the house.

"Well, I really don't know where to begin, but here goes." She closed her eyes. When had it all started? She recalled the day she first knew for herself, and when she talked to Sam about it. She was so scared that day, scared to lose someone who meant so much to her. She should have known it wouldn't matter to Sam. He had told her she was the same person, he just knew more about her now. He truly was an outstanding young man. Raynee opened her eyes and looked at Sam, "You remember Payton?" It was more of a statement than a question. She knew he would. Payton Mills was the last person she had had a relationship with. Sam had admired Payton. Raynee had fallen madly in love with her.

"Of course I do. Is that what this is all about?" Sam asked

tentatively.

"She called about a few months ago and we've talked on the phone several times since then." Raynee whispered as she attempted to hold back the tears. "She always asks about you." She gave him a cautious glance.

Raynee was quiet for a while as she reflected. She wasn't sure how Sam felt about Payton now; after all, it had been almost two years since she had walked out of their lives. Sam had witnessed the pain Raynee went through. He was very protective of his older sister. Could he forgive Payton for the agony she had caused? Was Payton trying to walk back into her life? Was she just trying to be nice? What did she want after all of this time? Did she know Raynee still kept her photo in her wallet? That she thought of her often....more often than she would even admit to herself.

Sam waited patiently for Raynee to collect her thoughts.

Raynee took her time, considering what to say before she continued. "She wanted us to get together," Raynee continued. "I finally agreed and we met for lunch last Sunday." Raynee relived the first phone conversation a few months before. Payton had called her on a Monday evening. As soon as Raynee heard her voice, her heart took one giant leap forward, then several short fast leaps. It had been a long time since she had heard that voice, yet with a simple "Hi," it all came racing back. She was flooded with sweet memories and heartbreak. Her mind raced. What did Payton want? Why was she calling now? Was something wrong? Did she still cherish the memories as Raynee did?

Raynee twisted her index finger around her hair, the way she always did when she was intent on what she was saying. Sam reached over and stroked her hair. "So how did the visit go?" Sam asked hesitantly.

"When we were together it was great. We laughed and reminisced. We talked a little about the split and the reasons why. I had a nice time and I think she did also. But when she left it really hit me. I didn't want her to go. I felt as though I was reliving the past, like she was walking out of my life again. Sam, I am so confused. I really thought I would be okay with being friends with her. But now I don't know. I'm afraid of her."

Sam's gentle expression quickly turned to anger. She placed her hand on his arm and quickly added, "No, she never physically hurt me. She wouldn't do that." The anger on his face was quickly replaced by confusion.

"Maybe I should have said I am afraid of me." Raynee lowered her head, unable to look into her brothers eyes. "I'm afraid of letting her get close to me again. I just can't go through losing her again."

"What about her problem and the reason she left? Rayn, you have to watch out for yourself." A tear rolled down her face as Sam lifted Raynee's chin. He smiled that big smile into her bright eyes. "Do you still love her?" he asked carefully.

"You know I never stopped," was all she could manage to say.

CHAPTER 2

The room was dark but she could see movement from the light underneath her bedroom door. What had woken her from her peaceful dream? The scuffle and muted screams that came from across the hallway caused her heart to beat wildly within her chest as she pulled the covers high. She could hear the furniture being thrown about the room, but couldn't force herself to move. She heard the voice then, a voice she hadn't heard in several months. But, the voice was different now. It didn't have the calming smoothness that had soothed her when she had nightmares. It was angry and cold. There was the sound of flesh landing hard against flesh, then she heard the cries of her mother, begging and pleading. The angry voice grew louder and then there was silence. She quickly exited the warmth of her bed and climbed into the back of her closet, hiding amongst the stuffed animals and other toys. She listened from the quiet confines of her safe hiding place, but all she heard was deafening silence. She stayed there until the sunlight illuminated her bedroom. Still she heard nothing from across the hallway. Clutching her stuffed rabbit, Mr. B, she slowly climbed out of the hiding place and slowly walked to the bedroom door. She pressed her small ear to the door and listened for several minutes. Hearing nothing, she carefully opened her door and looked into the hallway. It was empty and she couldn't see anyone in the living room. Slowly she walked the few steps to the open doorway of her mother's bedroom. Mommie was lying on the bed, still asleep. With a huge smile on her face, the small girl ran and jumped onto the bed with her mother.

The blood-curdling screaming coming from the small child forced Payton instantly wide awake. As she sat bolt upright, she realized she was drenched in sweat. She starting shaking and became conscious of the chill bumps covering her body from the cold, wet sheets. The sun had begun its gentle climb, awakening the new day. She threw back the covers and walked to the adjoining bathroom. Without bothering to turn on the light, she turned on the hot water and splashed the warmth onto her face. Slowly lifting her head, the eyes of the frightened child stared back from the mirror.

CHAPTER 3

When Raynee purchased the beach house four years before, she had turned the modest kitchen into one that was truly gourmet. She had added a bar between the kitchen and the living area, removing the confining walls, making a more open and welcoming area. She added industrial appliances and stocked the kitchen with all the things she would need for any creation. She hated to be in the middle of making a dish only to discover she didn't have a tool or appliance she needed. Yes, she was a kitchen gadget junkie. But since it was her favorite place to spend time in the house, she felt it was well worth the investment. She was undeniably her father's daughter.

She practically grew up in the restaurant her family owned. Her father had let her tag along in the summers when he opened the restaurant for dinner. She fell in love with the whole process and after graduating from culinary school, which her father had insisted she attend, she soon became head chef in the family restaurant.

Then that horrid evening a few years later, she and Sam had received the phone call they would never forget. Both of their parents had been killed by a hit-and-run driver. Sam was a senior in high school and Raynee had taken over the role of mother and father to him. Their parents' wills had left the restaurant to Raynee and the family home to Sam, and a hefty savings account for each of them. Sam, who was now attending law school, still lived there.

After their parents' death, the restaurant was never the same for Raynee. The memories of her father and their time there together were too much for her to deal with on a daily basis. After talking it over with Sam, Raynee sold the restaurant and invested some of the money into a place where she could relax and enjoy her downtime.

The beach house was the perfect place for her to get away from the city hustle and bustle. Because it was a relatively short drive from her city loft apartment, she spent as much time there as possible. Sam had use of the house whenever he wanted. They were all each other had and even if they hadn't been, she felt they would still share the same closeness they did now. They had always been friends, never the bickering siblings that were a part of so many families.

Raynee's latest venture was Pabulum, a restaurant she co-owned, so it didn't require her to work the horrendous hours she had after her parents' death. With losing her parents at such a young age, Raynee realized the importance of downtime and spending time with family and friends. She enjoyed her time off and arranged it so she could spend as much time as possible at the beach.

Looking around the house, Raynee remembered the first time she had walked through the front door. When she had announced to Chandler and Alex one night she was looking for a place at the beach, Alex had offered to introduce her to a friend of hers who was a realtor. Alex hadn't bothered to mention the realtor was drop-dead gorgeous.

A few days later Raynee received another phone call that changed her life forever. She remembered the sound of

Payton's voice over the phone, so sultry and alluring. They made an appointment to meet and discuss Raynee's needs. But during the meeting, Raynee felt her needs changing. As she listened to Payton talk about available properties, Raynee felt the need for this woman to touch her...to kiss her....to feel this woman. Raynee shivered at the memory. She had dated many women since she realized at fifteen she was a lesbian, but she had never felt this drawn to anyone before. How could Payton still do that to her? She felt the same warm tingling sensation now she had felt that day over four years ago.

So began the great house search. Payton would gather a group of listings and Raynee would quickly dismiss them. Raynee knew what she wanted and she was determined not to settle. As a result the two ladies start spending more and more time together looking at listings. After weeks of discounting numerous selections, one day Payton called and was bubbling about a listing she had just received for the perfect house. The current owners were friends of Payton's who offered her the house for the weekend. Raynee was dubious, but Payton was so adamant she agreed to look at it on one condition: she would drive down Saturday morning and had to return that evening. Payton had maintained a very professional decorum throughout the entire house hunting process. Alex had told her Payton was a lesbian, but she didn't feel comfortable spending the weekend with this woman she knew so little about personally, yet felt so drawn to.

Raynee followed Payton to the beach house. As soon as she pulled down the long drive and saw the house, Raynee had fallen in love with it. It was nestled at the tip of a small island off the coast of Georgia. The brick house with deep green trim was hidden from the road by the massive oak trees that covered the front yard. She immediately felt a sense of peace fill her as she entered the house. The inside was painted in soothing earth tones. Soft leather couches, which were included with the house, sat atop hardwood floors. The five-year-old home was in pristine condition. The current owners had it custom built and had enjoyed it until a job relocation had prevented them from visiting as often as they liked. The split bedroom floor plan had a large master suite on one side and two guest bedrooms on the other, each with their own bath. A small loft sat above the kitchen. It was separated by a half wall that overlooked the living area. It held a smaller bedroom and bath. A large living area had a wall of custom bookcases on each end. Nestled in the middle of the bookcase to the right was a small fireplace. The back wall was solid glass doors that overlooked a deck and pool which led to the private beach. Other than the changes she had made to the kitchen, the house remained basically the same as the first day she saw it.

Payton had been right. This was the perfect house for her. After the tour, Raynee had turned to Payton and was so excited she threw her arms around Payton in a huge hug and exclaimed, "This is it!" Then realizing what she had done, she quickly pulled away. The look on Payton's face was one of surprise and desire. Raynee felt her face turning red and she quickly stumbled over an apology. As she was trying to get the words out, Payton took a step toward her and placed a soft kiss on her lips. Now it was Raynee's turn to have the look of surprise and desire. They stood looking at each other for what seemed like minutes then slowly stepped into each others' arms for a series of passionate kisses. As hands caressed and the kisses became more hurried, they both realized what was happening and at the same time, they quickly pulled away from each other. Raynee recovered more quickly and said they should get all of the paperwork in place for the purchase of the house.

"I really have to get back." Raynee said, then quickly turned and practically ran out the door.

CHAPTER 4

The large glass doors were open, allowing the cool morning breeze of late August to blow inside. There he was on the sofa, deeply engrossed in a book. She snuck up behind the book and quickly snatched it from his strong hands, catching him off guard. Then with that laugh she was known for, she plopped down beside him. The echoes of her laughter flowed throughout the house. He looked into her smiling face and said, "Good Morning. It's good to see you smiling again." The smile started to leave her face when he grabbed her and playfully started to tickle her. He knew exactly where to touch her. After all, he had tickled her into hysteria so many times before. Raynee fell onto the floor, begging him to stop. He pretended to approach her again, extending his hand toward her.

"Okay, Sam, you win. Just please stop," she protested.

He knew not to push her. This was an especially hard time for her. He pulled her up from the floor and threw both arms around her. He affectionately kissed the top of her head. Her soft brown waves of hair tickled the tip of his nose.

"You're the best."

"Hey, that's what little brothers are for." he replied.

◊◊◊

By the time Chandler and Alex arrived, Raynee had prepared the ingredients for the grilled pizza and salads they would be having for lunch. Sam, of course, was a big help in tasting all of the pizza toppings to ensure their freshness as Raynee sliced the vegetables. Raynee popped him on the hand every time he grabbed another pepper or mushroom. "Would you please leave some for the rest of us?" she scolded him in mock protest. He just laughed and sat back in the barstool.

◊◊◊

After lunch on the deck, Alex suggested a walk down the beach. Sam commented it was either a walk or a nap. Raynee insisted he join them, so he cheerfully agreed. As they walked, the women took time to catch up. Chandler had been so busy with her catering business and Alex with her law practice, that they hadn't seen their friend in several weeks. Raynee avoided Sam's watchful eyes as Chandler commented that Raynee had lost weight and asked if something was bothering her. Raynee knew she would have to tell them eventually, but she would hold off until later. No point in getting Chandler upset right after lunch.

When Raynee and Payton had split up, Chandler was ready to beat some sense into Payton. She couldn't understand how Payton could leave someone as beautiful, kind, and caring as Raynee. What she didn't know and what Payton had hid from so many people was that she had an addiction problem.

Since then, Chandler had not seen Payton and rarely spoke of her. Chandler wasn't fooled by Raynee's avoidance of her questions, but like Sam, she knew Raynee would talk when she was ready.

In the distance, they observed a sailboat as it appeared to fall off the edge of the earth. Sam suggested they rent a boat and go sailing the following morning. Everyone was in agreement, so Chandler and Raynee started planning the picnic lunch they would take with them. Alex and Sam gave each other huge smiles and high fives, knowing how fortunate they were to have two chefs in their family.

As they continued their walk back towards home, the crew decided to spend the remainder of the afternoon on the beach. It was an unseasonably warm day, perfect weather for lounging in the sun.

◊◊◊

While the others prepared to hit the beach, Raynee mixed drinks for everyone. They met back in the kitchen and everyone claimed a frozen concoction and headed out the door. Just as Chandler and Sam walked onto the deck, Alex stopped Raynee and told the others they would be right out. Raynee looked at Alex with a puzzled expression. Alex peered over her shoulder to make sure the others were out of earshot then gave Raynee a warm smile and said, "I ran into Payton this week."

Raynee, tried to look surprised, "Oh, really?" She knew Alex and Payton talked occasionally and had remained friends.

"Cut the act, Raynee. We both know you're not an actress for a reason."

Raynee looked at Alex, her face blushing, knowing she was caught, "So, what did she tell you?"

"She said you had lunch last weekend. But don't worry, I haven't told Chandler yet. You know she's not going to be happy about this. She is so protective of you."

Raynee turned her head away from Alex, pretending to busy herself by wiping off the kitchen counter. Alex approached her, placing a hand on Raynee's shoulder. "I probably shouldn't tell you this, but I think she finally realizes what she lost. She has really gotten her life straightened out. She's been clean for almost two years. She hasn't dated anyone in quite a while. I really think she wanted to be sure of herself and her feelings before she attempted to contact you." Raynee looked up into the caring face of her friend.

Alex wiped the tears from Raynee's face and pulled her into her arms for a hug. "You know I can't keep anything from Chandler, so could you talk with her this weekend? Otherwise, she will hound me until I break once we get back home," Alex plead, then added, "Once she finished rehab and began therapy, Payton wanted to see how you were...to see if you hated her or would even agree to meet her to talk. I may be jumping the gun, but if you want to try to work things out with Payton, tell Chandler. She'll come around, but it may take some time."

Raynee knew Alex was right. Chandler had been there for Raynee through the breakup and as a result had formed a bond that would rival that of some blood relatives. Chandler was the sister she never had, and Raynee would need her support regardless of what happened with Payton. Once Raynee had composed herself, Alex grinned at her and said they had better hurry out before the others came looking for them. She slipped on her dark sunglasses to hide the redness in her eyes. She knew once she talked with Chandler she would feel better, but getting that conversation started was the hard part. Chandler was her best friend and they'd been through so much together. Chandler had been there for her and Sam when their parents had been killed. She was there when Payton entered her life and when Payton took a quick exit. Chandler was overly protective and wouldn't be happy to hear Payton was reappearing. But Chandler also knew Raynee had not been really happy since Payton left. Sure, she had gone out with a few people. Chandler had insisted on a few double dates, but no one was Payton.

◊◊◊

After a day on the water, the group returned to the beach house ready for a cool drink and a cold shower. Sam and Alex both volunteered to go first and retreated to their respective bathrooms. About that time, Raynee's cell phone rang. With a puzzled look at the number on the display, she answered the call. She recognized the voice instantly and felt the color drain from her face. The sultry "Hello" almost brought her to her knees. She tried to recuperate and was able to choke out a "Hi, how are you?" But when she glimpsed Chandler's face, she quickly turned her back.

Payton responded with a questioning, "Did I catch you at a bad time?"

Raynee, trying to sound as professional as possible, stated she was tied up at the moment and couldn't really talk, but could she return the call later. She feared that she wasn't fooling Chandler into believing this was a business call.

"Sure," Payton continued. "Call me at this number. It's my new cell phone number. I just wanted to see if you would like to go to dinner tomorrow night, but I understand it's short notice. Just give me a call later if you want."

"I um...I...I'll call you later."

"Okay."

Raynee knew her face must have lost all of its color. As she placed the phone on the counter, Chandler stepped in front of her and with a look of concern on her face asked if she was okay. "Sure, fine, why do you ask?" Raynee quickly turned her back, pretending to busy herself.

"Raynee, you look like you just saw a ghost."

Raynee knew Chandler had figured out something was bothering her, but she was sure she wouldn't suspect it had anything to do with Payton. Usually when something was bothering her, she always called Chandler. But she had just closed up and kept saying nothing was wrong. She knew she had probably appeared to be acting strangely. She had lost weight and she had been at the beach alone all week. The last time she had acted like this was when she and Payton had started having problems.

"I haven't seen you act this way since...Raynee, who was on the phone?"

Raynee tried to avoid looking at Chandler, as she knew the expression on her own face would give her away.

Raynee finally looked at the concern in her friend's face and knew now was the time. "I think we should sit down." She took Chandler's arm and led her to the plush sofa. Raynee sat sideways facing her friend who still had that please-don't-tell-me-what-I-think-you-are-about-to-tell-me look on her face.

"First of all I want you to listen to me and hear me out."

"Oh, geez Raynee, it's Payton isn't it. Now it all makes sense. The weight loss, you reverting back into your shell. Raynee, what are you doing? You know she is going to hurt you again. Haven't you been hurt enough by her? How long have you been seeing her? And why haven't you told me? You know that she is never going to change. Raynee, where is your head?"

"First of all, you need to calm down. Second, I am not seeing her. Third--"

"So what's going on then? That was her on the phone just now. Just try to deny it."

"Yes, it was Payton. We've spoken on the phone a few times and we went to lunch last Sunday."

"Geez, Raynee."

"Are you going to let me tell you or are you going to keep interrupting?"

"Okay, okay... I just can't believe this. Of all people, why her? I thought she was history. I thought you were finally over her. You haven't mentioned her name in so long. "

Raynee gave Chandler a stern look. "You're still talking."

With a scowl on her face Chandler pursed her lips, turned an imaginary key with the flip of her wrist and tossed the imaginary key over her shoulder. She leaned back in the corner of the sofa and glared at Raynee.

"Thank you," Raynee began. "I knew this was going to be difficult to talk about with you, which is why I have avoided it. But, here goes. Payton and I have talked on the phone several times in the past few months. Last week she called and wanted to meet me for lunch. I agreed and we met at Bridgewater Grille. We had a nice lunch and caught up on what was going on in each of our lives. We avoided the intimate personal information, both admitting we weren't in relationships and leaving it at that. We just had a nice, relaxing meal. Well, at least I tried to relax. It was so great to see her again. Chan, she looked so good, she was her old self, you know. She spent ten months in rehabilitation to get off the prescription pain killers, but she is clean and has been for the past year. She apologized for everything that happened at the end of our relationship. She explained a lot of things to me, like how she felt knowing she was lying to me by hiding the drugs. She also knew she had to make the decision to make the change and I couldn't do it for her. She has finally found the inner peace she was searching for. And she has faced her demons from her childhood. Chandler, she really has changed. Before you go jumping to conclusions, it was just a simple lunch. Nothing more...nothing less."

Chandler nodded her head slowly and quietly said, "We both know that isn't true. If that was all there was to it then why did she call again today?"

"I don't know….well…okay she asked if I was available for dinner tomorrow night. But, she just wants to be friends."

"Uh-huh, sure she does. And now she will start making plans with you every weekend, then it will be every few days…then she'll want you guys to tie the knot."

"Aren't you rushing it a little? You didn't ask me how I felt."

"Raynee Waters, I have known you for twelve years. You are my best friend. Do you think I can't look at your face and see you were thrilled to see her again? And you want more than a simple friendship"

"Okay, I was happy to see her again, but I am not ready to put a ring on her finger. Give me a little credit here. It was one meal."

"I don't know who you think you're fooling, Raynee, but it's not me!" the irritation growing in her voice as she got louder and louder.

Alex cleared her throat as she walked up in front of the sofa and slid into Chandlers lap. "So, you guys okay?" she said as she wrapped her arms around Chandler.

Chandler quickly looked back and forth at the two of them and shouted, "I should have known she already told you!" glaring at Alex.

"Oh sweetie, she didn't tell me, I ran into Payton Monday at the office. And get that scowl off your face." She placed her thumb on the wrinkle between Chandler's eyes and gently rubbed. "You needed to hear this from Raynee…not me." She placed her hand on Chandler's chin and gently pulled her in for a passionate kiss. Chandler seemed to resist, but it was clear that even if she was upset with her lover, she couldn't resist those lips.

Raynee took advantage of Chandler's distraction and ran off to grab a shower. As she stood under the spray, she felt some of her tension washing away. The talk with Chandler had gone better than she had imagined it would. Now, what was she going to do about Payton's dinner invitation?

◊◊◊

After a wonderful feast of fresh crab, shrimp, and lobster, the friends went to the deck to enjoy the cool breeze blowing off the Atlantic. After a few minutes, Raynee excused herself and went into her bedroom to place the call that had been on her mind since before her talk with Chandler. As the phone rang, she wondered if she was making a mistake, but she knew she wanted to see Payton again.

"Well, hello," came the seductive voice over the line.

How can she do that to me with a simple hello? Catching her breath she replied, "Hi, sorry I couldn't talk earlier. I am at the beach house with Sam, Chandler and Alex."

"So, how is darling Chandler? Does she still want to kick my butt?"

"Very funny." Raynee chuckled. "She's great. Alex told me she saw you this week."

"Yes, I hope she didn't say anything before you had a chance to tell Chandler we had lunch."

"I'm a big girl."

"Yes, but Chandler is bigger!" Payton laughed at her own joke.

"Not to worry. Alex is my ally." Not sure of how to continue, she finally continued, "So...um...is the dinner invitation still open?"

"Absolutely, unless you would rather make it another night since you probably won't leave the beach until the afternoon."

"I'm working nights Monday through Thursday, so tomorrow night is great."

"I'll pick you up at 7:00 then. How about Chinese? Do you still like Chef Tao's?"

"Sure, that's great. I look forward to it." Raynee felt the butterflies fluttering in her stomach and couldn't get the smile off her face. Payton was back in her life. "Look, I better go, I'm being a little rude to my guests. I'll see you tomorrow."

"Give Chandler my love, and tell Alex and Sam hi for me. I'll see you tomorrow."

When Raynee arrived back on the deck, she had a smile as wide as the beach. Sam and Alex both looked at her and burst into laughter. "What's so funny?" she protested. She could feel her face turning red and this time it wasn't from the sun. One quick look at Chandler told her she did not find this particularly funny. She had a snarl on her face.

"So what's for dinner tomorrow night….Raynee ala mode?" Alex snickered.

As Raynee playfully shoved Alex, they burst into laughter again. Chandler released a low growl and she rolled her eyes at the others.

"Well, I'm still not happy about this. She had better not hurt you again or she'll have me to contend with," Chandler grumbled.

CHAPTER 5

Payton pulled into the designated guest parking space for the loft apartments and took a deep breath. She had changed clothes four times before deciding on the black slacks with the simple white cotton shirt which was unbuttoned just enough to spark interest. Beneath it was a lacey black camisole. Black and pewter sandals completed her attire. Her light brown hair was cut short and naturally highlighted from the time she spent in the sun lately. She laughed at herself for being so nervous. She had spent two years getting her life back in order. For the first time in her life, she felt good about herself. She had eliminated her bad vices. Now the only addiction she had was exercise. Because of that, she was in the best shape of her life. The dark circles around her eyes were gone, as was the gauntness, and her deep brown eyes once again had a sparkle and her face a healthy glow.

She knew she had hurt Raynee when she left, but she also knew she would have hurt her more by staying. For several months prior to her leaving they had done nothing but fight. Raynee had tried to make her see what she was doing to herself, but she refused the help. She had refused to talk to a professional about the nightmares. The drugs consumed her life, temporarily dulling the pain. Then one morning after a particularly restless night, she had looked into the mirror and didn't recognize the person looking back at her. That was the day she realized she needed to do something. She had hit bottom and she was the only person who could do something about it.

Checking into the rehab facility was the best thing she had ever done for herself. She had to get her life back on track before she could totally commit her heart and soul to someone. Now she was finally ready to begin the next phase of her life. But what part would Raynee play in it? Was she even sure what role she wanted Raynee to play?

◊◊◊

As Raynee opened the door, Payton extended the single lavender and deep purple iris to her. Raynee blushed as she held the door opened for Payton to enter. "I picked it from my garden. I thought of you when I saw it." While she was in rehab, she discovered her love of and knack for gardening. As a result, she had a yard filled with lilies, roses, azaleas, and various other flowers and plants.

"It's beautiful...you remembered. Thank you." Payton knew irises were her favorite flower, and Raynee seemed touched Payton remembered. Motioning for Payton to have a seat, Raynee walked to the kitchen to gather a vase.

Payton took the opportunity to look around the loft. Her former home looked very different now. Raynee had totally remodeled since she moved out. Some of the furniture looked familiar, but the color scheme was different.

A welcoming foyer led to the combined living and dining areas. The kitchen was on the back wall, opposite the dining area. To the right of the kitchen was the guest bedroom and bath. To the left of the kitchen was the master suite. The master bedroom was now behind the new wall that ran the width of the loft. There was a large door on a sliding track to close the bedroom from the living area. She knew Raynee had wanted to put up a wall to create a more intimate area for the bedroom. The new wall was covered in bookshelves with the exception of the very center where a large television hung. New artwork adorned the exterior walls, surrounded by large floor-to-ceiling windows. The new colors were more bold and vibrant than the earth tones she remembered. She smiled sadly. Raynee had done a wonderful job with her home.

◊◊◊

When she walked back in the living room, Payton was looking around the loft. Placing the flower on the coffee table she followed the path of Payton's eyes. "I made a few changes."

"It looks nice, Rayn."

Raynee smiled at the nickname Payton often used. It felt nice to hear it come from those lips. Unsure what to do next, she tentatively asked, "Would you like to sit or are you ready to go?"

They looked at each other, exhaling at the same time, then they both smiled nervously. Apparently I'm not the only one nervous, Raynee.

"Either way...are you hungry?" As if on cue, Payton's stomach growled.

Laughing aloud, Raynee gathered her small purse from the table. "Apparently you are, so why don't we go?"

◊◊◊

After they were seated in the restaurant and had studied the menu, Payton ordered a bottle of Chardonnay.

After a few sips of the wine, Payton inquired, "How was

everything at the beach house?"

"It's really pretty there now. The weather was great. Sam came down and spent a few days and then of course, you know Chandler and Alex were there."

"How is Sam?" The two of them had gotten along well and Payton missed seeing him. "Is he still in school?"

"Yes, but he graduates in December. I am so proud of him. He is going to be an excellent attorney." The pride showed on her face as she talked about her brother.

"Alex said he might go to work with her?"

"They are still working out the details, but it looks like that's the plan." After a slight pause she added, "I told him we had talked. He asked how you were doing and sends his love. He really misses you. You should call him sometime. I know he'd like that," she added hesitantly.

She smiled at the tender face across from her, pleased with the suggestion. "I'd really like that. I'll call him soon."

Over platters of walnut shrimp and Mala chicken, Payton shared her latest ventures with her real estate business. She had been very fortunate to own the business with her mother's sister. While she was in rehab, her Aunt Janice had kept the business running smoothly. Now that Payton had her life back together, Janice was talking about retiring next year. Payton was a little apprehensive, but knew she would always be able to count on the occasional family assistance even after her aunt retired.

They both relaxed and laughed at each other as they used the traditional chopsticks to eat their meal. A few times, the conversation lapsed, but not in an uncomfortable manner. During these times, they both seemed to be caught up in their thoughts. While Raynee was wrestling with the chopsticks and a piece of chicken, Payton sat back and watched her. The determination on her face was so adorable. *She looks good, better than I remembered.*

After dinner they decided to walk off the meal and do some window shopping at the many antique stores and boutiques in the surrounding blocks. They came upon a jazz band playing on the deck of the pub down the street and stopped to listen for a while. When Raynee stifled her third yawn, Payton suggested she take her home.

The drive back to the loft was relatively silent. Payton walked her to the door. As she placed the key in the door, Raynee turned, "Would you like to come in?"

Payton hesitated slightly then replied, "No, you're tired and you need to get some rest." Then she reached across the distance and placed a soft kiss on Raynee's cheek. As she pulled back, she kept her gaze downward avoiding the searching eyes she felt looking at her. "Thanks for a lovely evening. And Rayn...I...I'm glad we can be friends." Then she turned and walked to her car.

◊◊◊

As she prepared for bed, Raynee struggled with her disappointment. She scolded herself for feeling that way. Apparently, Payton just wanted to be friends after all. What did she expect? Did she think Payton would just jump back into her bed? Did she want her to? *Well...it was a nice kiss,* she thought as she paced her hand on her cheek where Payton's lips had been just a few minutes earlier.

As she lay in bed tossing and turning, she thought of the evening and kept replaying those final words, *I'm glad we can be friends.* Yes, she admitted she did want more from Payton, but undoubtedly that was all Payton was able to give. Could she live with just being her friend after having been her lover? Was the love she felt for Payton capable of surviving a simple friendship? Yes, she cared that much...she had to or she would lose Payton forever. She would rather have a friendship with her than nothing at all.

She was awake most of the night going over the recent conversations with Payton in her head. She had to admit, not once had Payton indicated she wanted more. She had read into the conversation what she had wanted, not what had been conveyed to her. She was disappointed, but it was her own fault. She would have to put those feelings in the past and get on with her life. Something she probably should have done a long time ago. It was finally time.

CHAPTER 6

The screams filled her head...so loud, but where were they coming from? She lifted her hands to cover her ears. Make it stop...please make it stop. It was dark, so very dark, like all of the lights in the world had been turned off and the moon and stars had taken a vacation. She tried to move, but her legs wouldn't cooperate. Where was she and what had happened to her? Suddenly she heard the screams again....so loud...so very loud..then silence. I have to get out of here she thought. Once again she tried to move her legs, this time she jerked her legs free...and could feel herself falling.

Payton sat up with a start as she landed on the hard cold floor beside her bed. Her right foot was still tangled in the sheet she pulled from the bed as she fell. She tasted blood and put her hand to her mouth. "Bit my lip!" she exclaimed to no one. Untangling her foot, she stood up, brushed herself off and headed to the adjoining bathroom. Not bothering to turn on the light, she turned on the tap and rinsed out her mouth. The cool water stung as it hit her lip, but it did nothing to curtail the trembling she felt throughout her body. Grabbing her robe, she headed to the kitchen to start the coffee. She knew she wouldn't go back to sleep anytime soon. Glancing at the clock she grumbled. She had a meeting with a client at 8 a.m. She knew she would look like death warmed over, unless she could get a few more hours of sleep.

CHAPTER 7

The next few days were busy for Raynee as she planned the dinner specials for the week and placed food orders. Before she knew it, it was Thursday and she hadn't heard from Payton all week. Unsure of what to do with her upcoming two days off, she called Chandler on her cell phone. She answered on the third ring, sounding irritated.

"Hi, what's the matter? Are we having a bad day?" Raynee asked.

"No," Chandler replied, expelling a deep breath. "I just have to hire a new employee. Jess is moving back to Florida with her new girlfriend and we have a big catering job Saturday. She just told me today and she wants this weekend off."

"Look, I'm off for the next couple of days, I'll help you out."

"Oh God, Raynee, could you? Would you mind? I can get Alex, but you know how she is in a kitchen. I would really owe you one."

"No problem...I didn't have any plans anyway."

Chandler noted the disappointment in her friend's voice.

"So, have you heard from her this week?"

"You can say her name, you know."

"Yeah, yeah. Well, have you heard from her?"

"No, but I am sure she has been busy too." She wasn't ready to tell Chandler about the final words Payton had spoken to her Sunday night. She didn't want to hear an *I told you so*.

"Uh huh...Why don't we grab a pizza tonight and I can fill you in on the catering job?"

"I'm working tonight. Why don't I swing by in the morning with bagels and we can discuss it then?"

"Okay, come by the shop around 10:00. Have a good night. And Raynee...thanks."

As soon as she hung up the phone, it rang again. An impromptu party of twenty-five was looking for a place for dinner. It was going to be a long night. Raynee jumped up and started alerting the staff.

Raynee crawled into her bed at midnight completely exhausted. She hadn't slept well all week and it was finally catching up with her. But a few hours later when she glanced at her alarm clock, she knew it would be another restless night.

◊◊◊

Raynee spent all day Saturday assisting Chandler with the catering event. Raynee had told Chandler about the latest events with Payton the previous day when they were preparing the food. She had been supportive and seemed concerned about her friend. Chandler insisted she come over for lunch Sunday. Raynee readily agreed. She looked forward to some down time.

Sunday Raynee slept late, arriving at Chandler and Alex's

around noon. She had slept well last night and was looking forward to relaxing with her friends. It was a beautiful day, so she had the top down on her sports car. She was glad she had decided to wear the sleeveless V-neck shirt and shorts after all. The sun felt warm on her arms. As an afterthought, she threw her swimsuit into her bag. With the weather still this warm, she knew they would end up by the pool. Alex had insisted they install the pool the year before and Chandler reluctantly agreed, although Raynee knew they both wanted it equally as much.

As she pulled into their driveway, she saw a car she didn't recognize. She thought back, but couldn't remember Chandler mentioning anyone else would be joining them.

When Alex opened the door, Raynee noticed a strange grin on her face. Before she could ask what was up with her friend, Chandler appeared in the foyer with a blonde who looked a lot like Alex. Looking past Alex, Raynee and the blonde held each other's eyes for several seconds, before Raynee looked back at Alex with a questioning look on her face.

Alex jumped in, quickly making the introductions. "Raynee, I would like for you to finally meet my cousin, Lauren Tyson." Alex had spoken frequently of her cousin who lived in Texas. Then turning to Lauren, she continued. "Lauren, this is our dear friend Raynee Waters."

Lauren took a step forward and extended her hand. As she did, she flashed a smile and said, "It's so nice to finally meet you Raynee. Alex has spoken of you often and fondly." Her voice was almost a purr.

As Lauren grasped Raynee's hand, she gently rubbed her thumb across the back of it. Lauren gazed into her eyes, seemingly drawn into the way they sparkled. Raynee felt herself blush.

"It's nice to meet you." Raynee quickly pulled away,

feeling the burn of the hand. She didn't miss the wink Lauren gave her as she released her hand.

Chandler, oblivious to what was happening in front of her face proclaimed, "I'm starving. Let's eat!" Lauren broke her gaze from Raynee as everyone turned to Chandler and started laughing.

As they walked to the dining room, Alex put her arm through Lauren's and turning to Raynee said, "Lauren's moving to Atlanta. She was living in San Antonio, but has accepted a job with Emory University. She's going to stay with us for a few weeks until she can find a place of her own."

"Well, welcome to Atlanta. I've lived here all of my life. It's a great place to live," Raynee responded.

"Great, then maybe you can show me around sometime." Lauren smiled as she pulled out the chair next to her for Raynee to sit.

◊◊◊

Chandler had prepared grilled chicken salads with nuts, fresh fruit, and cheeses. Once the wine glasses were filled, Chandler proposed a toast to their guests. After the clinking of crystal subsided, they dug into the salads. Murmurs of approval filled the air. Chandler was pleased and it showed on her face.

"Alex, I don't know how you stay so slim with such a great chef in the house," Lauren complemented her hosts.

"The chef is sitting beside you," Chandler said with a grin on her face. "Raynee is the best chef in town."

Raynee once again felt herself blushing as Lauren turned to her. "Well, when do I get to sample your offerings?" Lauren winked at her as she flashed a smile once again. Raynee, who just took a sip of her wine, inhaled at exactly the wrong second, sending her into a series of coughs and sputters. Lauren quickly turned in her chair and started patting Raynee on her back. Raynee tried to pull away and in the process, knocked over her glass of wine which landed on Lauren's legs. Still coughing, Raynee grabbed her napkin and started dabbing at the wine-soaked, deeply tanned legs. By the time she realized what she was doing, she had stopped coughing. Looking up at Lauren, she started apologizing. Lauren reached across the distance, taking her hand. "Hey, don't worry about it. It's just skin, it'll dry." She smiled at the embarrassed woman. "Are you okay now?"

Tears welled up in Raynee's eyes as she quickly jumped up. "I have to go. Thanks for lunch."

Chandler quickly ran to follow her friend stopping her at the door. "Honey, what's wrong? It was just a glass of wine. It's okay."

"No, it's not okay. I have to go. I need to be alone now. I ..I...just need to be alone." Tears flowing down her face, she ran to her car and quickly drove off, leaving Chandler to wonder what had just happened.

Raynee pulled the car over to the curb when she was out of sight. What was going on with her? Why did she get so upset? And why did she run out on her friends like that? She was a tangled web of emotions. She had been alone for the past two years. Suddenly Payton had popped back into her life. She thought they would pick back up with their relationship. She hoped they would. *I'm glad we can be friends.* The words wouldn't stop playing in her mind. "Damn her!" she yelled as she pounded her fist on the steering wheel. Why can't you just let it go Raynee? And what was going on with Lauren today? She must think I am a total idiot. Running out and getting hysterical about a spilled glass of wine. *You had better get a grip girl because you are definitely losing it.* She pulled away from the curb and spent the next few hours driving around lost in thought.

◊◊◊

That afternoon as they sat around the pool, Lauren took the opportunity to learn more about Raynee. "So is Raynee always so emotional? Or do I just bring out the best in her?"

"She's just going through a lot right now. She's really a great lady and a good friend." Chandler beamed about her friend. "You just met her on a bad day. Give her another shot."

I'd like to give her more than that. Lauren recalled the first glimpse of Raynee at the front door earlier. *She is hot and not at all like I had imagined.* "Maybe I'll stop by her restaurant one day this week and talk with her." Lauren smiled to herself. *I think I'm going to enjoy these sweet Georgia peaches.*

◊◊◊

The ringing of the phone brought a startled Raynee out of her sleep. She had fallen asleep on the sofa after her long drive. Grabbing the phone, she pressed the talk button to stop the annoying ring. "Hello," she mumbled as she tried to wake up.

"Hi sweetie, it's Chandler. I just wanted to check on you. Are you okay? Did I wake you?" The concern was evident in her voice.

"I fell asleep on the sofa, but yes, I'm okay. I'm really sorry about today. I acted like a total idiot. I don't know what happened to me. I just lost it."

"No, you didn't, but we are all concerned. Do you want to talk about it? Is it Payton? Did something happen?"

"No, I just needed to be by myself. I think ...I don't know Chandler...I am feeling so many different emotions now and I need to get them straightened out in my head."

"Do you want me to come over?"

"No, I'll be okay. I think I'll take a long, hot bath and try to clear my head."

"Well, you know I'm here if you want to talk. Raynee, I love you."

"I know, and I love you too. I'll be okay...really." she replied, trying to sound convincing.

"I'll give you a call tomorrow. Good night." Chandler wasn't convinced, but knew Raynee well enough to know she would let her know when she wanted to talk.

"Night, and tell Alex and Lauren I'm sorry for running out so abruptly." She pressed the end button on the phone and walked to the master suite. A soak in the tub sounded really good.

CHAPTER 8

The lunch hour was in full force on Thursday. It had been a busy week and Raynee was happy to let the bustling energy at Pabulum keep her mind off of what was really bothering her. She liked the arrangement she and Sara, with whom she co-owned the restaurant, had. The ladies would alternate duties frequently, one running the kitchen, while the other ran the front of the house. Raynee loved to be in the middle of the kitchen when they were busy, but she found she also loved to walk the floor and talk with the customers. She had received valuable feedback over the years which they had incorporated into the business.

This week Raynee was running the front. As she walked to the lobby to check the wait list, she peered into the bluest eyes she had ever seen, only she had seen these eyes before. She was caught off guard when Lauren strolled up to her and said, "Hi."

"Um...Hi...What are you doing here?" Raynee didn't know if she was more embarrassed or annoyed. Why was Lauren here? She was working and didn't have time to socialize.

"I was hoping to grab some lunch, but if it's a problem, I

can go somewhere else." She was obviously hurt by the accusatory tone of the question. She turned to leave when Raynee put a hand on her arm. Turning back, she looked at the hand then up at Raynee.

Now Raynee really was embarrassed for having been so rude. Realizing she still held Lauren's arm, she quickly removed her hand. "I'm very sorry. I just wasn't expecting to see you here." Smiling, she added, "Of course you are welcome here anytime. Please, follow me."

Turning back to the maître d', she said, "Jeffrey, L4 is being seated now."

"Can you join me for a few minutes?" Lauren inquired as she took her seat.

"I'm really--"

Raynee stopped in mid sentence when Lauren lightly touched her arm. "Just for a minute, please?"

Without protesting further, Raynee took the opposing seat. "Look, I'm really sorry about the other day, I just have a lot on my mind right now and--"

"Raynee, you don't have to apologize. I was out of line with you. I don't usually flirt so openly with someone I don't know. But, I would like to change that. I mean the knowing you part. I'd like to be your friend."

The words hit her straight between the eyes. *I'm glad we can be friends. Why does everyone want to be my friend?* Trying to keep the irritation out of her voice, she stood up. "I'll get your server. Enjoy your meal."

.

Raynee stood behind the bar and watched as Amy took

Lauren's order. As Amy passed the bar on the way to the kitchen, Raynee stopped her and whispered something into her ear.

Minutes later Amy placed the glass of Malbec in front of Lauren, who quizzically glanced up, eyes following the hand placing the glass in front of her. "Compliments of the owner," came the reply to the unasked question.

◊◊◊

Raynee stood at a safe distance and observed the tall blonde as she obviously enjoyed her meal. She replayed the conversation she had with Chandler. Yes, she agreed it was time for her to start going out again. She hadn't seriously dated anyone in the past two years. She had only gone out a few times when Chandler pushed the issue. But no one really sparked her interest. Not like the woman she was looking at now. Lauren seemed to be interested in her too. At least she was interested enough to come here to eat and perhaps to see her. Twice she had been rude to this woman. She felt bad about her actions. It was time for a change.

◊◊◊

When it appeared Lauren was finished eating, she walked over to the table with a contrite smile on her face. "May I join you?"

Lauren looked up, seemingly unsure of how to take this woman standing before her. "It's your restaurant."

"Look, I'm really sorry about before...well, both befores. Can we start over?"

Lauren nodded toward the empty chair.

As she sat down, the server placed the check on the table, Raynee quickly grabbed it and placed it in her pocket.

"That's not..."

"I insist." Then with a pleading look in her eyes added, "It's the least I can do after the way I've treated you."

Their eyes locked as they sat smiling at each other, then for a split second Raynee saw the puzzled look cross Lauren's face. *Here it comes*, Raynee thought as she saw the recognition she had seen so many times before. She couldn't help but smile. Lauren picked up on it very quickly.

"Your eyes are beautiful. I don't think I have ever met anyone before with two different color eyes."

The smile extending even further, she said, "Thank you." Then before she could stop herself, she added, "Can I buy you dinner tonight?" *How can she do this to me? I don't even know her, yet I feel drawn to her.*

"You just bought my lunch." But as she saw the smile start to fade, she added, "But I would love to go to dinner with you."

"What if I pick you up at 7:00, we can grab a bite and I can show you around the city?"

"That's sounds wonderful. I look forward to it. But I had better run now. I'm looking at a few houses this afternoon. Thanks again for lunch." She flashed a smile and a wink as she looked Raynee over.

In a flash she was up and out the door. But not before Raynee had a chance to notice the exit from the rear and what a nice rear it was.

CHAPTER 9

Payton was sitting in her office when she heard the front door chime. Amber, the receptionist, buzzed her announcing her appointment had arrived. Payton walked into the lobby and extended her hand. "Hi, I'm Payton Mills. Let me grab the files and we can get started." Turning to her receptionist, "Amber, would you please get us a couple of bottles of water?"

Lauren took the extended bottle of water as Payton came back into the lobby. Payton scooped up the other bottle then shouted over her shoulder. "Lock her up when you leave. I'll see you in the morning, Amber."

As they walked out, Payton suggested they take her car and she could drop the blonde back by to pick hers up later. "Sure, as long as we can finish by 5:00. I have a date tonight."

"No problem, we should be able to cover these properties before 5:00." Then taking a long look at the lady sitting beside her, she couldn't help but think how lucky her date was.

"We'll start out in this area. I have a few houses I think you might like. They're located in the Ansley Park area close to Alex and Chandler, and to the University. We can look further if these don't suit your taste. I got the impression from our conversation last week you would like to live in close proximity to them."

"Yes, since my cousin is one of the few people I know in town and I like the area where they live. It seems like a great place to start."

While touring the homes, Payton began to get a better feel for Lauren's likes and dislikes. Pulling a small digital recorder from her pocket, she spoke into the microphone as they toured each property. She would review the notes later as she looked for additional properties. Her goal, as always, was to assist the client with finding the perfect home and she prided herself on being a matchmaker. Well, at least in home matching. Relationship matching was another story.

The pair talked casually as they went from house to house, with Payton pointing out features of each house. As they passed restaurants on the drive from property to property, she gave a mini review of each. Lauren watched the driver as she talked.

"So, do you live around here? You seem to know the area really well."

"Yes, not too far from here," Payton replied cautiously. She wasn't used to sharing personal information with her clients.

"Good, then maybe you can tell me if there are any good bookstores close by."

"Well, there's a Barnes and Noble not too far away."

Wondering if her suspicions about this lady were correct, she raised her eyebrow and a sly smile crept across her face. "That's not exactly the kind of bookstore I was talking about. I am more into women's studies, if you know what I mean."

Returning a knowing smile, Payton responded, "I know just the place. Charis Books is a local feminist bookstore and it's on

Euclid Avenue, which is not far. I think you'll find what you are looking for there." *So, she is a sister. Alex could have shared that little bit of information.*

As they arrived at each home, Lauren used her small camera to take pictures of the exterior and some key interior rooms. While Payton was locking up the last house, Lauren walked into the front yard and took a photo of the front of the house, capturing Payton in the photo as she turned to walk to the car.

"Digital cameras are the best. I can download these photos tonight to my laptop and look over them tomorrow between classes."

"Give me a call if you have any questions on anything you've seen. I'll go over my notes and pull some additional listings. Would you like to set a time to go out again?"

"Sure. I don't have any afternoon classes on Tuesdays. Are you available after 1:00 next Tuesday?"

Payton pulled the SUV into the parking lot at Mills Realty and checked the calendar on her phone. "That works for me. Would you like to meet here again?"

"How about if you pick me up at Alex's and then we can go out for dinner after we finish?"

"Uh...well..umm...sure...that's fine." Payton sputtered. She wasn't used to being so casual with clients. *Come on, give yourself a break, Payton. This is Alex's cousin and she's new in town. You could be nice and show her around. It doesn't mean anything.* Softening her tone, "That would be nice. Perhaps I could show you around afterwards."

"Then it's a date. Thanks for today. I think we are getting close to finding the perfect place." She turned and was out the door before Payton could respond.

Payton waited until Lauren pulled out, then turned her car toward home. *Maybe I'll give Raynee a call tonight. I haven't spoken with her in a few weeks.*

CHAPTER 10

When Lauren walked into the house, Alex looked up with a mischievous smile. "So, you have a date tonight. There you go using that Richardson charm again. How did you talk her into going out with you?"

"Ha...she asked me!" Lauren proclaimed proudly.

"Well, that's great. Just be careful with her. She hasn't dated anyone in a while."

"Hey, lay off, it's just dinner. Besides I like her, she's really cute...maybe a little strange, but definitely cute."

"Strange?"

"Yes, she almost bit my head off when I went to Pabulum today for lunch. She came back to my table later and refused to let me pay for my lunch. Then she asked me to dinner. Between today and what happened Sunday, which by the way I still haven't figured out, I would classify her as strange. Oh, and did I mention cute?"

"I think you mentioned it a time or two." Alex chuckled then added. "She's a great lady and of course Chandler will kill you if you hurt her best friend."

"I promise to be on my best behavior. I better grab a quick shower and figure out what to wear." Then with a quick flash of a smile, she was gone.

◊◊◊

Lauren chose a pair of navy slacks and a snug fitting light blue, V-neck blouse. She knew the blue of the blouse highlighted her eyes. She had finished dressing and was relaxing in the living room enjoying a glass of wine with Chandler and Alex when the doorbell rang. They all looked at each other, before Chandler announced she would get it.

She opened the door to see a very nervous Raynee standing before her. Stepping outside, she closed the door behind her. Raynee looked at her with obvious confusion.

"I just wanted to talk with you for a minute. Are you okay with this? I didn't mean to push you the other day, Raynee, but maybe it would help if you did start dating some. It doesn't have to be Lauren. I just think you should get out. Maybe meet some new people." The concern showed in her face as she looked into her friend's eyes.

"It's okay, you were right. I do need to get out. I've waited on Payton for two years and now I know she only wants a friendship. I have to get used to the idea. But, you're right. I like Lauren. She seems to be a very nice lady. Besides, it's only dinner."

"Now where have I heard that before?" she laughed at her friend, pulling her in for a big hug. "Alright then, let's get you inside. Your date is waiting."

As she entered the living room, her eyes caught Lauren's and she could feel herself flushing as her face lit up. Lauren held her gaze for several seconds.

"Hi," came the soft greeting.

God, she's adorable, Lauren thought as she looked at the brunette. She was wearing a silk beige blouse with dark brown slacks. The beige brought out the brown eye. This was a direct conflict to the green shirt she wore at the restaurant. The green brought out the green eye. Lauren chuckled at the realization. "Hi, yourself."

"Would you like a glass of wine?" Alex asked, breaking the ogling between the two women.

"Sure," she said, looking at Alex for the first time since entering the room. Then turning to Lauren, added, "Unless you're ready to go."

"Honey, will you help me?" Alex asked, capturing Chandler's hand as she walked past her.

"You bet." Chandler was silently amused at the response between the two women.

As they entered the kitchen, they both grabbed each other and started laughing. "Hey, this looks promising. Can you believe the way they are looking at each other?" Alex exclaimed. "I really think Lauren likes her."

"Well, Raynee seems a bit smitten herself. I just hope I didn't push her into this. I just hated seeing her get hurt by Payton again."

"Let's not rush anything. It's only dinner."

"What is it with everyone saying that? Look where 'just dinner' got us." She pulled Alex in for a passionate kiss. As they broke from the kiss she gazed into the eyes looking back at her. "Do you have any idea how much I love you?"

"Well let's kick them out of here and you can show me."

She placed a quick peck on her partner's lips and turned to pour the wine.

CHAPTER 11

"So, where do people who own restaurants eat?" Lauren said looking across the car at the lady beside her.

"At home." Raynee laughed as she replied. "But for you, I'll make an exception. What kind of food do you like?" She glanced to her right as she spoke. Wow, she thought, those eyes are incredible and that shirt really sets them off.

"I'm easy...I mean...I like all kinds of food." She choked out the response. "What's your favorite?"

"I know a famous place with great hamburgers, shakes, and fries. How does that sound?"

"Well...if that's what the lady wants, then that's what the lady gets. So, where is this famous place and does it have golden arches?"

"No, it doesn't. Have you ever heard of The Varsity? It's a landmark in Atlanta."

"Nope, but I'm willing to give it a try if you rate it so highly."

◊◊◊

Raynee let the top back on the convertible as they sat in the parking lot sipping their frosted orange and downing cheeseburgers and fries. "The Varsity is famous for their food as well as their chant, *What'll ya have?* People from all over the world come here to sit in their cars and place their orders over the speaker box, just like they did years ago. Everyone has to come here to eat at least once. The place actually opened in 1928. I have been eating here since I was a kid. Sometimes you just have to have your Varsity fix." She had to admit Lauren was being a great sport about this. She probably expected dinner in some fancy restaurant. But after a long week of working in the restaurant, she enjoyed relaxing with a good, old-fashioned burger.

"Well, thank you for exposing me to this place." She smiled as she spoke. Glancing at Raynee, she reached across the distance and wiped a spot of catsup from her cheek. Then she extended the finger to her own mouth, licking off the condiment.

Raynee watch the actions, not sure what to say. She felt her facing turning red and a flutter in her stomach. She quickly turned her head to look at the skyline.

"I'm sorry, did I embarrass you?"

"No, I love it when people groom me." She laughed as she stole a peep at a now-embarrassed Lauren. "So are you ready to see my city now?" she asked excitedly. Raynee was proud of the city and always loved showing it off to visitors.

They drove around for several hours with Raynee pointing out various points of interest.

"That's *The World of Coke,* a museum of the history of Coca-Cola. *Underground Atlanta,* over there is full of shops and restaurants. The *Fox Theatre* is a great place to catch a concert or play. It opened in 1929. She hoped she wasn't boring Lauren to death and was pleased when Lauren asked questions as they toured the city.

"So where do you live?" Lauren inquired as they headed back towards Alex and Chandler's house.

"I have a loft apartment not too far from here. It's small, but I like it. I've never been one for yard work, so the loft is great for me."

"I love to work in the yard. I usually plant a small garden each year. Just a few things like tomatoes and peppers. It's very therapeutic for me. Plus after teaching all day, it's nice to have an outdoor activity."

"I like to spend as much time as possible at the beach. That's my kind of outdoor fun. I also use Chandler and Alex's pool quite a bit. To hear them tell it, they each conceded because the other wanted the pool so badly. But, I know how much they both wanted it. Besides, it doesn't matter who wanted it as long as I get to use it too!" The laughter that followed seemed to echo as the car passed slowly through the city streets.

Before she knew it, they were pulling into the driveway and Raynee hated for the evening to end. She felt more at ease with Lauren tonight. The previous time they had spent together, she was stressed and uptight. Tonight she had relaxed and had enjoyed playing host. Looking over at Lauren, she saw the twinkle in her eyes when she smiled.

"Would you like to come in? It looks like the ladies are still up."

"I'd better go. I have to be at Pabulum early in the morning."

"I really enjoyed the evening. Thanks for the tour. I think

I'm going to like living here." As she opened the door to exit, she turned back and placed a soft kiss on Raynee lips. "See you soon I hope." She flashed a smile and a quick wink, then was gone before Raynee could speak.

CHAPTER 12

Raynee arrived at Pabulum the next morning to see a huge arrangement of fresh flowers on the bar. Sara looked up, smiling at Raynee from behind the bar.

"Wow, those are beautiful. You must have been a good girl last night," Raynee said grinning at her business partner.

"Actually, YOU must have been good. They're for you," Sara replied with a raised eyebrow and wicked grin.

"What? Who are they from?"

"Don't know, open the card and enlighten us both."

Raynee plucked the card from the vase. When she finished reading it, she turned red and quickly stuck the card into her shirt pocket.

"Oh, no you don't!" Sara protested as she reached across the counter and snagged the card. "Let's see what we have here." She made a show of opening the card, then proceeded to read aloud, "'*I had a wonderful time last night. I look forward to seeing more of you and less of your town next time. Are you available Saturday night?*' Well, well, this wouldn't happen to be from the striking blonde whose table you were sitting at the other day, would it?

"Give me that Sara. It was just dinner and besides we went to The Varsity, then I showed her around town. She's Lauren's cousin who just moved here from Texas."

"Well, you obviously made quite an impression. Maybe you should stay in Saturday night."

"I'll be here Saturday night. Remember you're off this weekend," she said throwing an irritated look at Sara.

"I'll work Saturday so you can go out with Ms. Hotty."

"No, you will not, you need your weekend off. Travis would kill both of us if you worked this weekend. You promised your husband a nice weekend together and he's been patient with both of us lately. Besides, I'll see her later....if I decide to see her again at all."

"Uh huh," Sara commented as she turned and walked into the kitchen.

◊◊◊

The dinner rush hour had not kicked into high gear when Raynee heard Sara talking to someone seated at the bar. As she walked closer she saw the familiar woman seated at the bar deep in conversation. Sara glanced up to see Raynee coming toward them and tossed her a big smile. Looking back at the lady in front of her she said, "There she is."

Raynee walked up to the adjoining bar stool and sat down beside Lauren. "Thanks again for the flowers, they're beautiful." Raynee had called Lauren at work to thank her, but had to leave a message since she was in class.

"Thanks for showing me around. I really enjoyed the

evening." Lauren placed her hand on Raynee's which was lying on the bar. "Look, I don't want to bother you. I'm waiting on Alex and Chandler. We're meeting here for dinner. I was just chatting with Sara while I waited." When Lauren noticed Raynee staring at their connected hands, she silently pulled her hand away.

Raynee looked into her eyes and felt the heat rising up her neck. She jumped up from the barstool then turning back, said, "I better get back to the kitchen. Enjoy your dinner."

With a puzzled look on her face, Lauren stared at the quickly disappearing form. Turning back to Sara, she shrugged her shoulders. "I don't get her," she said shaking her head.

Sara chuckled, "Well, I highly recommend you put some effort into trying to 'get her,' if you know what I mean. She's a great lady, she's just got a lot going on in that cute little head of hers right now."

◊◊◊

A few minutes later Chandler and Alex appeared at her side, each pulling up a bar chair. The bartender, Brian, recognized them both and threw them a smile as he poured two glasses of their usual wine. Placing the glasses in front of the ladies, he chatted with them about the new wines they had received. Brian placed a tasting in front of each of the ladies. Lauren watched in amusement as the three of them went into detail about the various aromas of apple, pear, vanilla, and nuts. It was easy for Lauren – she liked it or she didn't. She never could figure out the rich nutty taste lingering on your palate or the after tones of vanilla, blah, blah, blah...

Turning to Lauren, he asked, "And what are you picking up?"

With a quick raise of the eyebrows and a witty smile, Lauren replied, "None of the things you guys are talking about for sure. Obviously, I better stick to what I pick up best--hot ladies!" The group burst into laughter as the hostess announced their table was ready.

It helped to know the owner, because the three ladies got one of the best tables in the house. Their table was beside a wall of glass overlooking the Chattahoochee River. They sat Lauren so she had a perfect view of the manmade waterfall. The Oak and River Burch trees lining the banks were full of green leaves, while the hostas at their bases were a variety of greens and creams. The bright red hummingbird feeders flanked the bank on the opposite side were a source of amusement as the tiny birds zipped in and out grabbing quick gulps of the sweet nectar. A small bridge crossed this narrower portion of the river and a gravel-lined trail followed the banks as far as the eye could see in each direction. Often in the heat of the summer, canoes passed by Pabulum and the occasional canoer was known to stop by for a quick bite on the lower deck before continuing their journey.

After they were comfortably seated, Raynee stopped by with a wine chiller, a bottle of Chandler and Alex's favorite wine, and three glasses. Looking down at Lauren, she smiled and said, "This is the best I could do, we are fresh out of hot ladies." Caught off guard, Lauren looked Raynee in the eyes, but was completely speechless. This caused Alex and Chandler to almost fall out of their chairs as they rolled with laughter. Raynee turned, heading back to the kitchen.

"Quick one, she is," Chandler said when she could catch her breath. "Guess you have to be careful what you say around here."

Lauren just looked from Alex to Chandler with her mouth open, but no words would come out. *I just don't get her. One minute she's smiling that beautiful smile, the next she's upset with me. Then this....women – can't live with them, can't live without them.*

The ladies sat back and enjoyed the wine, each telling about their day and catching up on the activities for the upcoming weekend. Lauren had hoped to spend Saturday at the pool and then have a nice relaxing dinner with Raynee, although she left that part out of the conversation. The meals appeared in short order and they each exclaimed over the choices, which were all specials of the day. Raynee stopped by as they were finishing their meals and offered the dessert menus. Chandler just laughed, since she had made the tempting desserts herself earlier in the day. They each declined, but ordered coffee instead.

As Raynee turned to leave the table, Chandler touched her arm. "Can't you take a break for a few minutes and sit with us while we drink our coffee?"

Raynee quickly looked at Lauren, and seeing her smiling that sexy smile of hers, she accepted.

◊◊◊

As Raynee drove home that evening she replayed the evening and her interaction with Lauren. Sometimes she felt like such an idiot around Lauren. She went from happy to annoyed in minutes. She couldn't put her finger on it, but something about this lady got under her skin. She replayed the conversation between the cousins as she tried to figure out what it was. Lauren was fun to be around and obviously attractive. She had a great smile, fantastic body from what she could see. She was a professor, so she had it in the smarts dept. Why did she get to Raynee so much? Or – perhaps she should ask herself why she got so hung up on what Lauren thought of her or what she *thought* Lauren thought of her.

CHAPTER 13

Sunday evening, Payton picked up her cell phone, pressed the call log button then placed the phone back on the couch. She reached to pick it up again, but pulled back. She had left a message on Raynee's cell phone Saturday morning and hadn't heard back from her. *Is she ignoring me? Maybe it was a mistake to call her to begin with. I should have just stayed out of her life. Good grief Payton, it's only been one day. She probably worked all weekend. Don't be paranoid.*

Payton propped her feet on the coffee table and turned the television to a mindless reality show. She had been researching new real estate listings most of the afternoon after showing homes all morning. She suddenly realized she was very tired and closed her eyes for just a minute.

Mommie tucked her in bed and read her favorite story, the one with the bunny just like Mr. B. Wilber, the bunny in the story always took care of his girl, just like Mr. B always took care of her. He was her best friend. After she finished the story, Mommie lay down beside her and rubbed her back until she fell asleep. But the hand felt different this time; it was wet and sticky. She turned to face Mommie, but something was wrong. Mommie was covered in blood. Her screams pierced the silence.

The screaming wouldn't stop. It took Payton several seconds to realize it wasn't screaming she was still hearing, it was the sound of the phone ringing.

Grabbing the phone with one hand, she wiped the sweat from her face with the other. A quick check of the caller ID put a slight smile on her face. She tried to steady her breath, before pressing the answer button.

"Hi, how are you?" she said, while still wiping her face.

"Payton, what's wrong? Are you okay?" Raynee's voice was full of concern.

"Yeah, great."

"You know you are still a terrible liar."

"Well ..I ..uh...I ..had to run for the phone."

"Like I said, you are still a terrible liar. You know you can tell me the truth. It's not like I'm some stranger."

"I know, so how was your weekend? I guess you received my message yesterday. I was hoping we could grab a bite to eat tonight."

"My weekend was crazy busy. Sara and Travis went out of town for a few days, so I was running the restaurant solo. We had two huge parties yesterday and another one today. I wouldn't have called so late tonight, but it was the first time I have stopped all night and I didn't want you to think I was ignoring you."

"It never crossed my mind. So, when are Sara and Travis coming back?"

"Tonight. Sara insisted on working tomorrow and insisted I take the day off. I think I am going to sleep all day."

"Well if you wake up at some point tomorrow, would you like to go to dinner tomorrow night?"

"Well, a girl does have to eat, so sure. How about 7:00? Or do you have showings tomorrow afternoon?"

"No showings, so that sounds great. I'll pick you up at 7:00."

◊◊◊

Raynee arrived home much later than she expected. The large party at Pabulum had a hard time wrapping up their celebration. She immediately poured a glass of Chardonnay and began filling the jetted tub. She poured her favorite bath salts into the warm stream, stripped out of her clothing and slowly sank into the soothing water. The jets were positioned so they massaged the bottoms of her feet and her lower back. *How did I ever live without a tub like this?* After a nice long soak, she pulled herself from the tub, dried off with the plush beige towel, and fell into bed nude.

◊◊◊

After sleeping until almost noon, Raynee woke feeling totally refreshed and starving. Pabulum had been so busy the previous night she hadn't taken the time to eat.

Stretching as she righted herself, she pulled on a pair of shorts and an old T-shirt she had borrowed from her baby brother. She wandered into the kitchen and pulled open the refrigerator door. "Ahhh," she said as she smiled and pulled out a Sprite. She perused the contents and decided on a ham and smoked gouda cheese omelet. She grabbed a package of mushrooms, gave them a quick sniff and added them to the containers on the counter.

After devouring the omelet, she surveyed the room and decided it was in pretty good shape, so she picked up a book she had planned to get to for weeks, settled onto the couch, and spent the next couple of hours reading.

The ringing of the phone roused her from an unplanned nap and she gave a big stretch before checking the phone to see who was calling. She didn't recognize the number, but decided to answer anyway, since she was already awake.

"Hi, how are you doing this beautiful day?" came the soft voice over the line.

She didn't quite catch the voice, so responded with, "Who's calling, please?"

The chuckle on the other end of the phone was a giveaway. She instantly recognized the caller.

"Oh, sorry, hi. I didn't recognize your voice."

"I apologize, I should have announced myself." Lauren seemed embarrassed. "I was just surprised when you answered the phone. I expected to get your voicemail. Are you working tonight?"

"No, I'm actually off today and was just relaxing at home."

"Great, would you like to go to dinner tonight? I owe you after that fabulous burger you bought me last week."

"Hey now, I told you the Varsity is a must see if you plan to become an official Georgia girl," Raynee protested.

"I really did enjoy the company and the burger." The smile was obvious in her voice.

"Unfortunately, I can't tonight. I work tomorrow morning, how about you come by around 6:00 and I'll see what I can rustle up in the kitchen at the restaurant for an authentic Georgia meal?"

"That sounds great. I'll see you tomorrow. Enjoy the rest of your day."

"Until tomorrow." Raynee realized she was smiling as she disconnected the call.

◊◊◊

Raynee felt a surge of energy after the conversation with Lauren. She jumped up, changed into her workout clothes, and went to the gym in the building. She ran on the treadmill, reviewing the conversations she had with Payton over the past several weeks. She relived the day she met Lauren and the time they had spent together. She thought about her life and her future. She thought about Sam and she thought about her parents. When she finally stopped running, she was exhausted and soaked in sweat.

Raynee went back to her loft and stripped her soaked clothing off her wet body. She got into the shower and wept. She wept for the parents she lost at such a young age. She wept for the events that had pushed Payton to drugs to kill the pain. She wept for the mother Payton had lost as a young girl. And she wept because the hurt in her chest needed release. As the water began to cool, she felt her tears began to subside. The pain she had felt, all of the emotions she had held in for the past few months, somehow seemed lighter now. She turned off the water and began to dry her body with the soft, warm towel. Why did crying lift a weight from your chest, but completely drain you at the same time?

◊◊◊

It was almost 7:00 and Raynee was still trying to decide what to wear. After looking through her closet for the fifth time, she finally decided and just added her earrings when the doorbell rang. After a quick check of her selection, she hurried to open the door.

Payton, appraising her from head to toe, smiled that beautiful smile as Raynee stood at the open door. Raynee felt her heart leap. "Wow, nice outfit Rayn. That blouse looks great on you."

Raynee felt herself blush as she shrugged off the compliment. "Thanks, you look rather lovely yourself."

"Are you ready?"

"Sure, let me grab my bag." she said as she turned to grab her purse from the couch. When she turned back around, Payton was staring at her. She had seen that look before. Her breath hitched and she stopped for a second. She slowly let out her breath and walked back to the door. Payton kept her eyes locked on her the entire way. When she got to the door, Payton reached up, brushed the tips of her fingers over her face, then leaned down and gently kissed her on the lips.

"Let's go," Payton said as she took Raynee's hand to lead her down the hallway.

◊◊◊

They shared a bottle of a Meritage wine while waiting on their entrées to arrive. The conversation was casual as they both seemed lost in thought.

Raynee kept remembering the kiss and how Payton's lips had felt. It was such a soft kiss, she wasn't sure it had actually happened. But the beating of her heart as she reminisced assured her it had indeed occurred.

They ate in comfortable silence, listening to the local artist sitting on the small stage playing the guitar and singing. Occasionally he would stroll through the restaurant, stopping at random tables to sing a special request for the diners. He stopped by their table right as they were finishing their meal. When he asked if they had a request, Raynee shook her head, but Payton requested one of Raynee's favorite songs, "The Way You Look Tonight."

Neither of them knew quite where to look as the artist sang. Raynee kept stealing glances at Payton, but Payton kept her eyes fixed on the candle burning between them. When he completed the song, Payton thanked him and handed him a few bills. Only after he had walked away did Payton look at Raynee.

"Thank you for doing that." She tilted her head indicating the musician. "It's one of my favorite songs. My parents loved to dance to it."

"I remember you telling me. I also remember you playing it on special occasions, like their birthdays and their anniversary. I hope you enjoyed it and it didn't bring up bad memories for you."

"Quite the opposite. It makes me happy to hear it and think of them."

"Rayn, I know I put you through so much when I left and when I wouldn't talk to you before things got so bad. I live with that guilt every day and I really need for you to know I truly am sorry. I hope one day you can forgive me so I can forgive myself. You mean so much to me and I hate the fact that I hurt you." There was sadness in her eyes and the pain she held onto was reflected in her words.

Raynee was taken aback by Payton's sudden confession. Although they had shared several meals over the past few months, they had danced around the breakup and the impact it had on each of them. "It was a tough time for both of us. I'm glad you were able to get professional help. I hope you know I have guilt as well. I feel guilty I wasn't able to see what was going on with you so I could help you."

"It wasn't your place to help me. I was the master of denial. I know you kept trying to get me to talk to you, but I was in a place I didn't want to share with you, a place so dark I couldn't share it with anyone. I hope you can understand. The addiction had nothing to do with you, but it did have a lot to do with my childhood. Rehab helped me to learn how to better deal with it. Attending the Narcotics Anonymous meetings helps too. Just know I am very sorry and please don't feel any guilt. You have absolutely no reason to feel guilty. Do you think you could ever find it in your heart to forgive me for what I did to you...and to us?"

"I forgive you," Raynee replied with the utmost sincerity, her eyes whelming with tears.

"Thank you. That's all I needed to hear."

◊◊◊

The walk back to Raynee's loft was quiet, except for the occasional comment about a display in a shop window. Raynee felt a sense of peace within she hadn't felt in quite a while. Although she never felt it necessary, she found it odd just saying the words, "I forgive you" made her feel lighter.

When they arrived at her front door, Raynee turned to thank Payton for the evening. When she looked up, she saw such sadness in Payton's face. She silently prayed she would find total peace one day. She reached up and placed her fingers on Payton's cheek, Payton leaning into the contact. Looking directly into her eyes, she simply said, "I'm always here for you. More than anything I wish you would let yourself be happy."

Payton gave a slight nod, took Raynee's hand in hers, kissed her palm then turned and walked away.

CHAPTER 14

Her cell phone rang just as Raynee was about to walk out the door of her loft. She dropped back down on the couch when she saw the name on the caller id. "Well, hello."

"Hi yourself. Did I catch you at a bad time?" Lauren inquired.

"Nope, I was just heading to run some errands, but I'm in no hurry. What's up?"

"I am going to take a second look at a house this afternoon. Alex was supposed to go with me, but had to cancel at the last minute. I wanted to see if you were available. I just want a second opinion before I make a decision. This is a big step for me." Hesitantly she added, "It shouldn't take too long and then I'll buy you dinner afterwards if you like."

"When were you planning to go?"

"Sorry for the short notice, but in about an hour if that's okay with you."

"Your timing is great. Sure, I'd be happy to go with you." She was genuinely pleased Lauren asked her.

"Oh Raynee, thank you so much." Her relief was apparent.

"How about I pick you up in about 30 minutes? Can you be ready then?"

After providing the address and parking instructions, Raynee added, "I'll see you shortly."

◊◊◊

Lauren and Raynee were having a lively conversation when they approached the house. Raynee's eyes were drawn to the house and she didn't notice the person standing beside the car in front of the house. They were still laughing as they exited the car. Raynee rounded the front of the car to see Payton standing a few feet away. Payton looked at Lauren and then over to Raynee, then back again.

Raynee let out an audible gasp then mentally kicked herself. Of course Payton would be her realtor. The thought had just never crossed her mind. It wasn't that she didn't want to see Payton. In fact, she had left Payton a couple of messages after their last dinner, but Payton had never replied. She was unsure of how Payton would react to seeing her, especially with Lauren. It didn't take her long to find out.

"What are you doing here?" Payton's tone was harsh as she glared at Raynee.

"Oh...um...do you know each other?" Lauren looked from one to the other, and she seemed genuinely surprised.

"We have a history," Payton said bluntly.

"I'll wait in the car while you take a look around, Lauren." Raynee turned to walk back to the passenger's side of the car.

"Wait, Raynee, that's not necessary, both of you come in." Payton's tone was a little gentler this time.

Lauren looked from Payton to Raynee. She truly didn't

70

understand the anger she felt resonating from Payton. "Okay, let's go then," she said, not too sure what was going on.

Payton unlocked the front door and stood back to let Lauren and then Raynee pass. She raised her hand to catch Raynee's arm, then lowered it. "Take your time and look around. I'll be outside if you have any questions." She turned, closing the door behind her.

"Raynee, I'm sorry, I didn't know you knew Payton. We can go and I can do this another time. She doesn't seem to be happy to see you."

"It's a long story. Let's take a look around. I'll fill you in later when you buy me the glass of wine I'll need."

They strolled from room to room, Lauren pointing out her likes and occasional dislikes, Raynee offering occasional suggestions. Fortunately the dislikes could be rectified by a little paint and minimal work. It was in Inman Park, which was only a couple of miles from the University where Lauren taught. The house was a chalet bungalow, which was adequate space for a single person. There were two bedrooms, two baths, a living area, a dining room, and an upstairs loft area that would make a great guest room or office. A small nook perfect for a breakfast table was just off the kitchen. To the right of the nook was a set of French doors which led to the backyard. The backyard was a showpiece. Obviously the current owners enjoyed outdoor living. There was a screened-in porch which ran the entire width of the house. From the porch extended a patio which edged a kidney shaped pool. Beyond the pool was a beautifully landscaped yard. The backyard living space was twice the size of the house itself.

Lauren told Raynee that Payton had explained a couple had bought the house and spent a lot of time working on it, then decided to have a baby and didn't feel it was safe to have a pool and a baby, so they had bought a larger home farther from the city.

Taking it all in, Raynee exclaimed, "Wow, this is amazing! If I didn't already have a place, I would buy it myself."

"Do you really like it?" A smile spread across of her and her eyes twinkled. "Isn't it the greatest?" The excitement was evident in her voice.

"Absolutely, especially the outdoor space. You should be able to use this almost year round." Turning, her eyes caught a structure off to the left. "Wow, it even has a built-in fire pit."

"I'm going to make an offer. I just wanted to see if someone else would agree with me. I was totally smitten the first time I saw it, but you know how sometimes when you take a second look it isn't as great as the first time you saw it. I think I love it even more after seeing it through your eyes. Thanks for coming with me. I owe you big!" Lauren was beaming as she reached in and wrapped her arms around Raynee's shoulders, giving a slight squeeze before releasing her.

They both turned to go in search of Payton, who had walked onto the porch in time to see the embrace. Raynee glanced up to see the hurt expression on her face and just as quickly saw her professional demeanor reappear.

Lauren was too excited to notice and immediately began talking about making an offer on the house and bombarding Payton with questions.

Glancing at her watch Payton said, "I have to meet another client in a few minutes, so why don't I write up the offer tonight? Can you swing by tomorrow to sign it?"

"Sure. That would be great. I'll come by before my first class. It 8:30 okay with you?"

"That's fine."

"Raynee, let's get out of here so Payton can get to her next appointment." Turning back to Payton, she said, "Thanks for letting me see it one more time. I know I'm making the right decision."

CHAPTER 15

Payton hated lying to Lauren about having another appointment, but she had to get away from the two of them. What was Raynee doing with Lauren anyway? Lauren was trouble; she should have detected that right away. She was a flirt and was after anything with boobs. She would have to talk to Raynee. Raynee deserved better than someone like Lauren, and she would make sure she knew what kind of person she was. She was certain she was right in her assessment - there were girls like her all over - she just had to make sure this one stayed away from her Raynee. She would finish the sale of the house and she would be professional, then she hoped never to see the likes of Lauren Tyson again.

Payton pulled away from the house and headed for her favorite local bar. She sat at the bar and had a few drinks while she chatted with Mandy, the bartender. She watched the various ladies walk in and out, but none of them caught her attention. Not the way Raynee did. She loved Raynee and one day she would be ready to build a new relationship with her. She knew she wasn't ready yet, but she would be one day. Surely Raynee knew how she felt and was willing to wait for her.

◊◊◊

Payton poured herself another bourbon when she arrived home. She hadn't eaten today, but the bourbon was filling the void and besides it tasted better than some random microwavable dinner for one.

She sat on the couch and picked up the remote, flipping through channels until something caught her attention. Nothing did, so she turned down the volume and laid her head back.

The light was so bright she couldn't see anything. It was as though a spotlight was in her face. She flailed her arms around trying to get the light out of her face, but it wouldn't go away. It was too bright to be able to see the source. She closed her eyes.

The screams were so loud. Why was she screaming? She touched her arms and legs but felt nothing. She wasn't hurt, but why the screams? Just stop...please stop...you're making my head hurt....JUST STOP SCREAMING!

She opened her eyes again, but there was only the light and silence.

Payton jumped at the sound of the ringing. Before she could gather her wits about her enough to realize her cell phone was ringing, the annoying tone stopped. She lifted her hand to her face and wiped the tears away. Looking at the missed call, she didn't recognize the number. She would check her message later. She reached for her drink...she would need more to get through this night.

CHAPTER 16

Two days later, Raynee's phone rang as she was leaving Pabulum.

"Are you busy tonight? I need someone to celebrate with and I was hoping that someone would be you." Lauren was obviously beaming.

"May I ask what this celebration is for?" Raynee teased. "And yes, I am free tonight"

"You are talking to a new home owner!" Lauren was bubbling with excitement

"Lauren, that's great! In that case, I'm treating you to dinner. Or....I was planning on cooking for myself tonight, would you like to come over for a home-cooked meal instead?"

"Are you sure you don't mind the intrusion? Or we could just do it another time...I mean I don't--"

"Stop – come over around 6:30 or 7:00. That should give me plenty of time to get to the store, get home, and get everything ready."

"Thanks Raynee, that sounds wonderful. I look forward to seeing you. I'm just so excited. I can't wait to get settled in my new place. Once I do, I'll invite you over for dinner." As if suddenly realizing who she was talking to, she tried to backpedal. "Oh...wait...never mind. I'm not cooking for you EVER...you're a chef, what was I thinking?" Lauren laughed.

Raynee chuckled at Lauren's obvious excitement. "Once you get settled, I would love for you to cook for me. I'm really easy to please. I mean I'll eat just about anything...I mean, not to say that your cooking isn't good, I am sure it is, but don't be intimidated to cook for me just because of my occupation." Raynee felt like she had just stuck her proverbial foot in her mouth. "I look forward to seeing you tonight. I'll pick up some Champagne to toast the special occasion. See you soon."

◊◊◊

Raynee stepped in from her deck just as the doorbell rang. She took a quick glance around the loft to make sure everything was in place and ran to open the door. A beaming Lauren was standing there holding a beautiful bouquet of flowers.

"These are for you," she said as she extended the bouquet.

A similar smile spread across Raynee face as she gathered the flowers and breathed in their aroma. "Thank you, but you shouldn't have."

"You were gracious under fire the other day. It's the least I could do." She tilted her head and winked.

Raynee felt herself blush as she stepped back to allow Lauren entry.

"This place is beautiful Raynee." She politely walked around the living space taking in the view from the various angles. "You must love living here with all of this open space."

"It's comfortable. I do like the openness most of the time. But then when you have people over, you can't just stick everything in a room and close the door." Raynee laughed nervously as she spoke.

"I highly doubt you are a messy person based on what I know about you thus far."

"Would you like the nickel tour? Come, let's get a glass of wine first." She headed toward the kitchen and stopped in front of a large wine chiller. "What would you like? We're having grilled salmon salads for dinner."

"You're the expert, I'll take whatever you suggest." She walked over and peered over Raynee's shoulder at the contents. "Now, that's a wine chiller."

"Thanks, I bought it from the company that sells us equipment for the restaurant. He made me one of those you-can't-turn-it-down deals, so I didn't." Grabbing a bottle, she placed it in the countertop wine opener and pulled down the handle to extract the cork. She reached up to the rack and pulled down two red wine glasses and poured a taste into one. She offered the glass to Lauren. "Try this and let me know what you think."

Lauren took the proffered glass, gave the wine a swirl and took a sip. She swished it in her mouth for a moment, then swallowed. "Yum, that is wonderful. Filler up!" she requested as she held the glass out.

Raynee laughed at her dinner guest as she poured each of them a generous glass of the Pinot Noir. After a tour of the loft, which took all of five minutes, Raynee seated Lauren at the bar while she finished preparing the fish for the grill.

Lauren watched Raynee and she worked quickly to slice the salmon into filets. She observed her hands and the fluid movement of the knife skills. Her eyes began to travel up her arms. *Nice arms and shoulders.* Her eyes continued their journey to her neck and then down her chest to the top of her shirt. The V-neck form-fitting shirt offered the slightest peak at her cleavage. *Really nice chest.* Her eyes roamed over the firm breasts and down the slim waist. As Raynee bent to pick up a baking sheet from the lower cabinet, she caught a peak of the lower back and her small nicely shaped rear. She licked her lips and caught herself when a low moan passed her lips.

Raynee turned around. "I'm sorry, what did you say?"

A red-faced Lauren quickly fibbed, "Oh, I was just thinking about my new home."

Raynee let it go, because she had felt Lauren's eyes on her while she worked. She liked the feeling it gave her and didn't want to dissuade Lauren. She found herself becoming more and more attracted to her the more time they spent together. She had been pleasantly surprised when Lauren had asked her to go with her to look at the house and especially pleased she called her today after getting confirmation the house was indeed hers. She knew she needed to give her an explanation about Payton. She hadn't wanted to talk about it that night after they left the house, and Lauren hadn't pushed it. She was still upset with Payton about her reaction, and knew she would have to talk with Payton about it eventually.

"Let me put this fish on the grill, I'll be right back."

"I'll come out with you, it's a nice evening." Standing, she picked up her wine glass and walked around the counter to gather Raynee's. "What else can I take?"

Smiling as she looked into her eyes, Raynee replied, "It looks like you have the most important things." Then very uncharacteristically of her, she winked at Lauren.

Lauren could hardly contain the smile which spread across her face and she followed Raynee to the deck.

As they ate, they chatted about the house. The closing was scheduled for a short four weeks away. Lauren had already made a list of the some of the things she wanted to do right away and a second list of a couple of changes she would make later, after she was settled. She was very animated in talking about her new home. Raynee sat back in her chair, sipping her wine as she watched with amusement the joy abounding from her dinner companion.

Raynee offered to assist in any way she could and Lauren quickly accepted the offer. "I want to repaint the master bedroom and the dining room. Will you go with me to pick out colors?"

"Absolutely, just let me know when you are ready." She picked up the bottle of wine and refilled their glasses. "Let's go sit in the living room where it's more comfortable."

"Let me help you with the dishes first." She reached over to pick up the oversized salad bowls when a hand stopped her. Her eyes followed the hand up the arm to Raynee's eyes.

"I'll get that later, there's not much to do. I want to talk to you about Payton." The smile had left her face and she suddenly felt sadness enveloping her. "I owe you an explanation."

Looking into her eyes and sensing the mood change, Lauren replied, "You don't owe me anything. If you want to talk about it, I'll listen, but you don't have to."

"No, I really want to." she took Lauren's hand and led her to the leather couch. She sat at one end with her back to the edge, slipped off her shoes, and put her feet up. Lauren followed her lead and placed her own next to Raynee's, their legs touching. Raynee picked up the remote and turned on a soft jazz station.

Not really sure where to begin, she looked tentatively around the loft, then to the woman sitting across from her.

"Payton was my realtor when I bought the beach house about four years ago. We started dating shortly after the closing. She moved into the loft with me about six months later. I know that's years in the lesbian world, but we were both being cautious. Anyway, about a year after she moved in things started to decline. The housing market was not great and her business dropped. Payton carries a lot of baggage from her childhood.

"When she was small, her parents split up. According to her Aunt Janice, they had a tumultuous relationship, to put it lightly. Payton lived with her mom, but saw her father occasionally. Something happened one night, they still aren't sure what, but Scott, her dad, snapped. He came to the house where Payton and her mom lived. It was late and Payton was asleep, although she remembers the loud argument between them waking her. She hid in her closet, like she always did when they fought. The next morning, she ran to join her mother in bed..." Raynee looked up, tears flowing down her face. "Her mother was dead."

Lauren looked shocked at what she was hearing. "Poor Payton. That's horrible. No child should have to endure what she went through."

"She's had nightmares about finding her mother most of her life. They had stopped when we first got together and she always gave me credit for them stopping. I think...no, I know, we were both very happy in the beginning. Anyway, the nightmares she had started up again. When that happened, she started pulling away from me. We started arguing more, but I chalked it up to the stress we were both under. I didn't realize how bad it was until I came home one day and found a note on the table and all of her things gone."

"She just left? I can't imagine what you've both been through."

"She had become addicted to pain pills and was checking herself into rehab. I didn't see, or didn't want to see, the signs for a long time. I knew she was depressed about her business and attributed her actions to that. I tried and tried to get her to talk to me or to talk to someone, but she refused. She became belligerent every time I mentioned it. She started staying at her office later, or at least I thought that's where she was, but later I found out she was at a bar. She started drinking more and more. Then the day I found the note, I realized how bad she really was. She was away for almost a year. I hadn't heard from her or seen her since the morning she left. In fact, we just reconnected this summer a few months before I met you. That's why I was a basket case when I first met you."

"I had no idea."

"I know and I'm sorry I didn't tell you before. It's so hard for me to talk about. It's a very private matter."

"I'm so sorry you had to go through that."

"It wasn't all bad. We had a few good years together. I think the trauma from her childhood was just too much."

"So she came back into your life about the time I met you? No wonder you were so emotional, you had a lot going on."

"Yes. We've had dinner a few times, but nothing more. She's made it clear she just wants to be friends. At first I was really hurt, but now I know it's better this way."

When she stopped talking, Raynee looked over at Lauren. Her head was down. The moon was bright enough for her to see the tears pooling on her folded hands. Raynee tentatively reached across and wiped the tears from her cheek. As she did, Lauren looked up at her.

"So why do you think she was so upset when you showed up with me at the house this week?"

"I don't know. I haven't spoken with her about that, but I need to." Raynee let out a deep breath, feeling totally drained.

Lauren reached over and placed her hands on Raynee's. "I'm sorry for your pain and I'm sorry I put you in an uncomfortable position the other day." Gently rubbing the hands she held, she continued. "Thank you for telling me."

Raynee looked at their joined hands and then at Lauren. She saw the compassion in the eyes looking back at her. "Thanks for listening and for understanding."

"I know you did everything you could. But you couldn't fix her past. She had to deal with it herself. Turning to drugs to ease the pain was not fair to you or your relationship. You are such a good person. I know she is an important part of your past and I understand that. Thank you for sharing with me. I promise you everything you told me tonight will go no further."

Lauren started to reach for Raynee, but held herself back. "Would you mind terribly if I held you right now?"

There was such tenderness in the question, Raynee could only nod. She slid over between Lauren's legs and placed her head on her chest. When she felt strong arms wrapped around her, she leaned closer to her chest. The two sat in silence, Raynee relishing the strength of the beautiful woman holding her, Lauren admiring the strength of the woman in her arms.

◊◊◊

Raynee woke the next morning feeling euphoric. She hadn't felt so comfortable in the presence of a woman in a long time. She was also glad she was able to talk with Lauren so honestly the previous evening. It felt good to just get everything off her chest.

As she showered, she began to think about Payton and her attitude at seeing her with Lauren. She knew they needed to talk. She also wasn't looking forward to the conversation. Payton had quite the temper. Tossing ideas back and forth in her head, she decided to just call her and get it over with. Payton was the one who wanted them to be "just friends." If she was jealous of Lauren, she would have to get over it.

She was the first to arrive at Pabulum, so she went to her office and placed the dreaded call. She was relieved when she received voicemail. She left a brief message asking Payton to return her call. Pleased she made the gesture, she sat back in her chair and began her work day. The ball was now in Payton's court as to whether or not she wanted to call her back.

CHAPTER 17

Thanksgiving was coming up soon. Their annual tradition was for Raynee and Chandler to cook for Sam and Alex. Occasionally they invited others to join them. Since Sam and Lexie had been dating, she joined them. Some years it was at Raynee's loft, sometimes at Chandler and Alex's house, and occasionally, weather permitting, they would take advantage of the long weekend and all go to the beach house for several days.

Raynee hadn't spoken with Chandler about the plans for this year, but she knew Lauren would be included and she was excited about that. The two of them had been on several dates, but hadn't been intimate yet. Not that it hadn't been on her mind, but Raynee was in no hurry to jump into bed with just anyone, and she felt she and Lauren were really getting to know each other. Since Lauren was her best friend's cousin by marriage, it could turn awkward if things didn't work out between them. Therefore, she preferred to keep going at a slow pace and not fall into the stereotype of bringing the U-Haul to the second date. While it was on her mind, Raynee grabbed her phone and pressed the speed dial number. Chandler answered on the second ring.

"Hi sweetie, what's up?" Chandler answered.

"I was just thinking about Thanksgiving and wanted to start making plans. Have you guys talked about what you would like to do this year? I was thinking the beach, since Sam and Lexie graduate in December and with him just starting to work, it may be hard for all to get back down there for a while. Also, since Lauren is here now, she may want to join us, unless she is going back to Texas for her break. But I didn't know if you guys would be able to go down for the long weekend since you have both been so busy lately. I feel like I haven't seen you in ages. I just--"

"Slow down tiger! Take a breath." She laughed aloud. "Thanksgiving is like two months away, so no, we haven't really talked about it yet."

"I just didn't want to wait until the last minute." she protested.

"Look, I can tell you are ready to put the plans in place, so why don't you come over tonight for dinner and we can all talk about it."

"I can do that, but will..um...do you think Lauren will be there?" Raynee and Lauren had both been so busy lately, they hadn't seen each other in a few weeks. She knew Lauren was still getting settled into her new house.

"Do you want her to be?" she asked, amused with Raynee's obvious nervousness.

"Yeah, sure, yeah, that would be fine."

"Raynee, honey are you okay?"

"Yes, I guess. I'm just excited. So much is changing in our lives this year and I just want it to be a great holiday season for everyone."

"It will be, I promise. Besides, Sam isn't moving away after graduation. He'll still be here working in the firm with Alex."

"I know. I'm being silly." Raynee breathed a small sigh. "Okay, let's talk about it tonight. I really want to make it special for Sam."

"You're thinking about your parents, aren't you? How they won't be there to see him graduate?"

"How do you know me so well?" Raynee replied, tears forming in her eyes.

"That's what best friends do. We have super powers that allow us to read minds. Sometimes we are even able to predict the future and I predict a wonderful Thanksgiving surrounded by wonderful friends and great food, regardless of where we are."

"Thanks Chan, you are the best friend a girl could ever have." Her sentiment was filled with love.

"We will all be there for Sam to make sure he has the best graduation ever."

"Okay, I'll see you guys tonight. Love you, mean it!"

"Love you, too. Bye."

◊◊◊

Raynee arrived to find Lauren's car parked in front of Chandler and Alex's house. She grabbed the two bottles of wine she brought and hurried to the front door. She had her fist up to knock when the front door sprang opened. She looked up into the most beautiful eyes she had ever seen and couldn't contain the smile that filled her face.

Lauren perused the length of her before inviting her to come in. "Wow, you look great. It seems like it's been ages since

I've seen you." Leaning over, she placed a kiss on Raynee's cheek.

Raynee wanted to reach up and touch the spot where Lauren's lips had been, but held back. Instead she regarded Lauren before replying, "Right back at you. How's the house coming along? Are you settled in yet?"

Raynee stepped inside and Lauren closed the door but made no attempt to move into the house.

"I'm getting there. The truck from Texas arrived last week, so it's starting to look more like a home. I still have boxes here and there to unpack, but it's livable, finally."

"I can't wait to see it." Raynee smiled at the tired but seemingly very happy Lauren.

"Give me another few days and I'll feel comfortable having company. At least now you'll have a place to sit."

"Hi stranger," Alex said as she met them in the foyer. She reached in for a big hug from Raynee. "Yum, you brought the new wine we tried at the restaurant," she added taking the bottles from Raynee and walking toward the kitchen. "Come on, let's get this party started."

Lauren and Raynee laughed as they all made their way to the kitchen where Chandler was putting the finishing touches on dinner.

"Wow, it smells yummy in here," Raynee exclaimed as she gave Chandler a hug and a kiss on the cheek.

"Just grilled vegetables and chicken breasts. I'm testing out a new marinade recipe I came up with, so I expect honest feedback. If everyone is ready to eat, the food is done now." Chandler picked up a platter and pointed to the other with her chin. "Can one of you grab that platter?"

Lauren and Raynee both reached for the platter at the same time, but Raynee was a split second ahead of her and was picking it up as Laurens hand reached hers. Their hands touched and Raynee felt a jolt of energy that almost caused her to drop the food. She made a slight gasping sound and looked up to see what she felt was the exact expression on Lauren's face that was on her own.

With a nervous smile, Lauren pulled back to allow Raynee passage to the dining table. Raynee chuckled to herself when she heard the gush of air Lauren released as she walked to the adjoining room.

◊◊◊

"Okay, do tell what you used in your marinade Chan, because this is amazing," Raynee praised. The murmured agreements resonated through the room as mouths were busy tasting the meal.

"No can do lady, I'm thinking about creating a line of grilling sauces and marinades. I think grilling is the absolute best way to cook a meal. Why don't more people take the time to learn to grill something besides the occasional burger or steak, which more often than not is cooked to death and ruined? Grilling is an art and has to be mastered."

"She has turned the kitchen into a mini lab lately, trying this and that. I can't say they were all winners, but she has several now that are outstanding. Add this one to your list babe. It is yummy!" Alex exclaimed as she placed another bite of chicken into her mouth.

"Chan, have you ever…" Raynee stopped to think though the idea that popped into her head. "What if you taught grilling classes and used your products? You could charge for the classes and sell your products."

"Um, did you forget about the catering? I don't have time

to teach classes too," Chandler proclaimed.

"But what if you had a partner and you had a facility where you could teach and cater instead of the small building you use now for the catering?"

"Did you have someone in mind?" Looking across the table at her friend, a small grin spread across her face.

"What if we did it together?" the excitement evident in her voice.

"Did you just have yourself cloned, because the last time I looked you were staying pretty busy yourself with Pabulum."

"I've been thinking..." Raynee's minded wondered and she thought through the possibilities.

"Uh oh, hang on. Raynee has been thinking. This will be good. Fill us in." She loved to give her friend a hard time.

"Very funny. You know Chelsea is an excellent chef and she has been talking to Sara and I about becoming a partner. So, I was thinking of bowing out and starting a new business. I had no clear idea until now about what I wanted to do. Why don't we open a cooking school?"

"That sounds like a great idea, Raynee. Is there anything similar around here?" Raynee had apparently piqued Lauren's interest.

"We'll have to do some research to see who our competition would be or if there is anything like that around this area, but we could always put a different spin on it to make us unique."

"I like the idea so far, but we need to do a lot of research. We would have to find a facility to accommodate a large group with lots of outdoor space." Chandler's eyes were lighting up at the possibilities.

Chandler turned to Alex who nodded her head in agreement. "I think you guys should definitely do your homework. I've never heard of anything like that around here. I'll ask around too just to see what I can find out."

"It sounds like you guys have some work to do. I'll be glad to assist in any way I can," Lauren chimed in.

After agreeing they would investigate the possibility, everyone, consumed with their own thoughts, continued eating their meals.

Raynee sat back and looked around the table. She felt such a sense of pride sitting there among these people. Alex and Chandler meant the world to her and now Lauren was starting to play an important part in her life as well. She felt the love and warmth surrounding her and her eyes began to tear.

Lauren happened to glance over at Raynee about that time and saw a single tear roll down her cheek. Concerned, she placed her hand on Raynee's arm. "Are you okay?"

"Just very happy," was all she could manage to say.

◊◊◊

After the scrumptious dinner, they filled their wine glasses and adjourned to the deck. The wide expanse of outdoor living space extended into the back yard where an inviting pool lay. It was a beautiful night with a crispness in the air indicating fall was well underway. Lauren sat on the glider and patted the cushioned seat beside her for Raynee to join her. Chandler and Alex sat in a patio chairs to their right.

"So Raynee, let's talk about Thanksgiving. What did you have in mind for this year?" Chandler opened the conversation.

Looking first at Chandler and Alex and then at Lauren, Raynee explained how this chosen family has always spent the Thanksgiving holiday together and some of their traditions, as well as including Lexie now that she and Sam were dating. "I told Chandler I really wanted to make this year special for Sam. He graduates in December and I know it will be hard for him with Mom and Dad not being there. Of course, you are invited to join us this year if you don't have plans. We just need to see what everyone has going on, but I would love to go to the beach house if everyone can," Raynee rattled on nervously.

"That sounds like fun! School is out the week before Thanksgiving, so I'm in, regardless of where we go. Mom asked me about coming back to Texas, but I didn't want to go back so soon. I was just there a few weeks ago to complete my packing and the move."

"Chandler, Alex — what about you guys? Does your schedule permit a long weekend at the beach?" Raynee asked, looking to her friends.

"I can definitely do it, how about you honey?" Chandler said, looking at her partner.

"I'll have to let you know closer in, but let's plan on it and I'll try my best to be there. If I can't make it for the whole weekend, then I should be able to swing it at least for a day or two. Have you checked with Sam yet?" Alex asked, looking back to Raynee.

"I called him last night. He said he was up for whatever we girls decide. You know where there is food, there will be Sam." Raynee chuckled.

"Is he still dating Lexie?" Alex inquired.

"Yes, he and Lexie are still dating, but both seem more focused on finishing this last year in school than they are in being in a serious relationship. I think that may change once he passes the bar exam and Lexie has her CPA exam out of the way."

"I've never met your brother, but have heard so much about him. I look forward to meeting him." Lauren seemed genuinely excited about the upcoming holiday.

"You'll love Sam. He's like a little brother to all of us," Chandler chimed in. "Plus he is really nice – not sure where he got that from."

"Hey now!" Raynee protested. She knew Chandler was teasing her and she also knew how much Chandler loved Sam. He was a great brother and was adopted by her family by choice as the little brother to all.

"I can't wait! Thanks for including me." Lauren looked over at Raynee as she spoke the words, their eyes locking for several seconds, until Alex's coughing brought them back to the conversation at hand.

Raynee felt her face getting hot as Lauren withdrew her gaze.

"Anybody need a refill?" Alex held up the bottle of Viognier they had been drinking.

"I really need to go. I have a ton of things to do tomorrow and I don't need to have a wine hangover," Raynee explained as she stood up.

"I'll walk you out. I need to get home too." Lauren grabbed both wine glasses from the side tables as she walked into the house, joined by the others.

"Lauren, when are you going to invite us over to see your new place?" Alex inquired. She and Chandler had been over a few times during the unpacking process and assisted her but had not seen it in about a week.

"How about I have all of you over next weekend?" she pointedly looked at Raynee as she asked, a smile crossing her lips.

"Sure, that sounds great. What can I bring?" Raynee looked into Lauren's eyes as she spoke. There was a softness in her expression Raynee hadn't noticed before. She gazed at those gorgeous lips and gently bit her bottom lip. When she looked back up at Lauren's eyes, she knew she was busted. She felt her face turn red, but she couldn't stop the smile spreading across her face.

"Just yourself", then on second thought she added, "Unless you want to bring some of the delicious wine we had tonight." She reached out and touched Raynee's arm. "I'll walk you out."

After a round of hugs and goodbyes, Raynee and Lauren walked to Raynee's car. She unlocked the door and as she turned to open it, a soft hand stopped her. She looked at the hand and then slowly looked up at Lauren standing within a foot of her. As she caught her eyes Lauren leaned forward and kissed her very tenderly. Raynee wasn't sure where the moan came from, but as Lauren pulled back, Raynee took her arm and pulled her back to her lips. Raynee reached up and ran her hands through Lauren's hair, something she had wanted to do all night. Lauren wrapped her arms around Raynee's waist and pulled her back to her waiting lips as the kissing intensified. Raynee opened her mouth to allow Lauren access. She didn't waste any time accepting the invitation. As their tongues began their exploration, their hands caressed each other. At the same time, they both saw the front porch light go off and on several times, flashing like a strobe light. They released their hold on each other and both burst into laughter.

"I think we just got busted," they said in unison and both looked up to see Alex and Chandler standing at the open doorway, laughing.

"Night girls," Chandler called as they waved, then turned and closed the door. The light went off immediately afterward.

"You know we'll never live this down," Raynee said gazing into Laurens eyes.

"It was worth it." Returning the gaze, Lauren smiled back at her.

"I agree. As much as I hate to, I really need to get home. I had a wonderful time tonight and I look forward to seeing your place next weekend." She leaned in and slowly kissed Lauren, wishing the entire time it could last for hours.

CHAPTER 18

Raynee arrived at Lauren's new home Saturday afternoon. She gathered a large basket and tote bag from the trunk and made her way to the door. Just as she was trying to balance the packages to free a hand to ring the bell, the door opened.

A beaming Lauren looked down at the packages and relieved Raynee of the bag. "Come in, it's great to see you." Raynee followed her, taking in the khaki slacks clinging to her slim hips. The ocean blue button-up shirt was loosely tucked in. She smiled when she realized Lauren's feet were bare.

Raynee placed the oversized basket on the kitchen counter. An eager Lauren stared at it in amazement. "That is the largest gift basket I have ever seen." She chuckled. "May I open it?"

Raynee laughed at the stunning woman before her. Sometimes she could be so childlike in her excitement. "Of course, it's yours."

Lauren took the end of the large bow and gently pulled it, her eyes locked on Raynee. It was the most seductive thing Raynee had ever seen. It was as though Lauren was undressing her instead of the basket. She could feel the butterflies in her stomach as the paper fell from the sides of the basket. She bit her bottom lip and turned her eyes from Lauren. *Oh my Gosh, I am in so much trouble with this one.*

Lauren yelped as she slowly began pulling the contents from the basket. "Raynee this is incredible." she exclaimed as she pulled three bottles of wine, several types of gourmet cheese, assorted boxes of crackers, a slate cheese tray, cheese knives, four wine glasses along with several bottles of olives, sundried tomatoes, pesto, and olive tapenade.

"Well I couldn't decide, so I just kept adding items." Shyly, she looked at Lauren. "I hope you like it."

"What's not to love? Thank you so much!" She leaned in and wrapped her arms around Raynee. She held her for a little more than a basic friend hug would last. When she pulled away, she turned her head and placed a warm kiss on Raynee's lips. The kiss was eagerly returned.

"Mmm...I'll bring you a basket every time I come over if I get a thank you like that." They still held each other as they gazed into each other's eyes.

Lauren placed another kiss on her lips before taking a step back. "I think I need a drink," she laughed as she turned to the counter where an open bottle of wine sat in a chiller along with four wine glasses. Handing the filled glass to Raynee, she took her by the arm and began to walk her through the house. "Let me show you what we've done."

The pair walked through the house, Raynee admiring the changes. The living area was a deep khaki with crisp white crown molding. The colors complimented the hardwood flooring and the blue pillows piled on the leather couch. An inviting fireplace covered the wall opposite the couch and was flanked with a hearty natural wood mantle. Down a short hallway was the guest bedroom and bath, again painted in earth tones. The bedding was light green with warm beige trim. Again, accent pillows decorated the bed. In the corner was an antique rocking chair overlooked by a dark metal floor lamp. Landscape portraits covered the walls.

"Those photographs are beautiful." Raynee admired the artwork closely.

"Thanks, I took those a few years ago when I went to Wyoming." She smiled as she ran her finger over the frame. "I remember the sounds and smell of the mountains the morning I took these shots. It was such a perfect day, one that brings such great memories every time I look at the pictures."

"You took them? Wow! Did you ever consider going professional? You have a great eye," Raynee continued, impressed.

"No, it's just something I do for pleasure. I have done some private work for my friends Shea and Jillian back in Texas. Shea wanted a nude of Jillian for their bedroom. It took her a while to talk me into doing it, but they were very pleased with the results. "

"Wasn't it weird taking nude photos of a friend?"

"Not really. Shea was there and explained what she wanted. I've known them for years. I felt honored she trusted me to do the work and Jillian is so comfortable with her body that she was a natural." Reaching out, she took Raynee's hand. "Let me show you the rest."

"If I didn't know better, I would never guess you just moved in. This place looks great. You even have artwork on all of the walls."

"I don't like bare walls. I wanted to make it look and feel like a home as soon as possible. To me, it's not a home without those simple touches."

"You have a great eye for detail. I love it." Raynee continued her perusal.

When they arrived at the master bedroom, Raynee felt those butterflies in her stomach again. It was such an intimate space, she felt shy about walking in with Lauren's hand in hers.

The room was accented in green with the same earthy walls. The queen bed was covered in a light blue and beige comforter. At least a half dozen pillows of various shapes and sizes covered it. A beige chaise lounge chair extended from one corner of the room. A stack of books was on the table to the left, which also held a reading lamp. An oversized television graced the wall opposite the bed and chaise. Other than that, the room was void of furniture.

Raynee looked around the room, noting the obvious omission of vital furnishings. Just as she was about to ask, Lauren opened the door to the left. Raynee's mouth fell open when she gazed into the massive walk-in closet.

"I did make a couple of changes in this room," she said, extending her hand towards the closet.

"Wow! This is the kind of closet you read about in designer magazines," Raynee exclaimed as she turned, taking in the contents. The wall on the right held one row of hanging rods, while the opposite wall held two rows to accommodate pants and blouses. In the center, a cabinet at least eight feet long contained shelves and drawers on either side. The wall at the back of the closet was covered in shelves that held dozens of pairs of shoes.

"Well, a girl has to pamper herself." She laughed at the shocked look on her guest's face.

"Amazing!" was all Raynee could manage to say.

As they walked back into the bedroom, Lauren pointed to

the new door she'd had installed which led to the back patio. She opened the door and took Raynee's hand as she led her to the backyard. They strolled around the yard hand in hand, sipping their wine while Lauren told her about the loft area she was using as an office/library.

The conversation was interrupted by a familiar pop song. "I think your pocket is singing." Raynee chuckled as Lauren released her hand to extract the phone from her pocket.

"Hi sweetie, what's keeping you guys? Oh, okay. No, it's okay. I hope she feels better soon. Give her my love and take care of her. Okay. Love you, too."

Turning to Raynee, she said, "You probably got the gist of the conversation, but Chandler is not feeling well so they won't make it tonight."

"Does she need anything? Is there anything we can do?" Raynee asked.

"No. She has a stomach bug, so she isn't eating right now. Hopefully she will be okay by tomorrow. So, I guess you get me all to yourself tonight." She winked at Raynee and took her hand again as she led her back into the house.

◊◊◊

Lauren retrieved a baking dish from the oven and placed it on the kitchen table beside a tray of assorted crackers and various types of cheese. "Spinach dip," she announced, leaning over to refill their wine glasses.

Raynee grabbed a cracker and dipped it before taking a bite of the combination. "Yum. Did you make this?" she asked, quickly grabbing and dipping another cracker.

"Yes, as a matter of fact I did." She beamed.

"I thought you couldn't cook."

"I never said that."

"You said you wouldn't cook for me."

"Exactly, but apparently I lied since I cooked dinner for you tonight." She chuckled. "I'm not very good at it, but I do enjoy playing around in the kitchen. There are a couple of things I cook fairly well, I've been told." She winked at Raynee and then shot her a grin.

"So what do you like to cook?"

"Lasagna, which is what I made tonight."

"Double yum."

"You haven't tried it yet," she teased.

"If it's half as good as this dip, I will love it. I love Italian food."

Lauren just smiled at her without responding.

Puzzled at the expression, Raynee asked, "Why did you cook lasagna tonight?"

"Because Alex said it was your favorite."

Raynee reached across and popped Lauren on the leg. "Cheater."

"Hey, a girl's gotta do what a girl's gotta do. I always heard the way to a woman's heart was through her stomach."

After a dinner of lasagna, breadsticks, and salad, the two sat back in their chairs rubbing their stomachs.

"You can make lasagna for me anytime. Dinner was fabulous."

"I'm pleased you enjoyed it." Lauren beamed.

"No, you don't understand. That's the best lasagna I have ever eaten," Raynee admitted.

"Now you're just being nice." She smiled at the compliment.

"No, I am very serious."

"Wow, that's a huge compliment. Thank you very much." She stood and took a bow, a huge smile covering her face.

"Let me help clean up."

"No, I'll do it later, let me just put the food in the fridge. Maybe I'll take some to Alex and Chandler tomorrow."

"I'll help, I need to work some of this food off."

"Okay, if you insist. Bring our plates in if you don't mind," Lauren said as she walked to the kitchen.

They made quick work of the clean up, working well in unison. When the dishes were washed and the food put away, Lauren held up the wine bottle and extended it towards Raynee's glass. "Would you like more wine?"

"Sure, just a little."

"Would you like to sit outside? I have the fire pit ready to build a fire?" Lauren asked.

"Oh, that sounds nice." She gathered their wine glasses and followed Lauren to the backyard. "It's so beautiful back here. I would stay out here all of the time if I lived here."

"I do love it back here, but this is the first time I've really been able to relax and enjoy it without feeling guilty about unpacked boxes glaring at me through the windows."

Lauren had a roaring fire going in no time at all. As she continued tinkering with it, Raynee sat back and enjoyed the view of the stunning woman who obviously knew her way around a campfire. She lay her head back on the chair and closed her eyes, enjoying the smells emanating from the fire. She felt a tickle on her nose and reached up to scratch when she heard a soft chuckle close by. She opened her eyes to see Lauren's face only inches away. Her breath caught as she looked into her eyes. Lauren leaned in as Raynee's hand captured her cheek. Their lips met and Raynee felt a twinge in her southern regions. Lauren dropped to her knees between Raynee's open legs as the kiss intensified.

As she pulled back slightly, Lauren hummed. "You looked so beautiful sitting there, I couldn't resist."

Lauren's hands were on either of the armrests and Raynee covered them with her own, her fingers rubbing delicately over Laurens forearms.

"Dance with me," she requested as she stood and offered her hand to Raynee who silently accepted the request.

The music faintly flowing from the house set the pace for a slow dance as their bodies joined. Lauren was slightly taller, so Raynee rested her head on her shoulder as they moved. They danced together like they had done it for years, Lauren moving her hands up and down the length of Raynee's back as they swayed back and forth. Raynee rested her hands around Lauren's neck, running her fingers through her hair.

"Ummm...that feels nice." Lauren leaned into the touch.

Turning her head up, Raynee placed her lips on Lauren's. The kiss was soft, even gentle, until Lauren lifted the back of Raynee's shirt and began to stroke her skin. The kiss intensified as Raynee opened her mouth slightly. Lauren brushed her tongue over her teeth. Lauren backed them up until her legs hit the edge of the chaise lounge. Holding onto Raynee, she lay down, pulling her on top of her length.

They continued the kiss as their hands journeyed, discovering new parts of each other. Raynee pulled her lips from Lauren's and trailed down her neck and to the top of her chest. As she slid her body down to have better access, she felt a jolt run through her body and moaned at the sensation. Her hands, then her lips trailed the front of Lauren's shirt, only stopping when her lips felt the hard nipple. Gently she nipped through the blouse, realizing the bra Lauren was wearing was rather thin. Lauren arched her hips as Raynee's lips curled around her aching breast. Raynee reached down, unbuttoned the shirt, and pushed it back for better access. Tracing her fingers over the lacy bra still covering her goal, she smiled broadly when she opened the clasp on the front of the bra releasing the most gorgeous breasts she had ever seen. She placed her face in the cleavage as Lauren pressed her breasts together with her upper arms. Raynee continued her journey, this time traveling to the previously ignored breast. Lauren moaned as Raynee flicked her tongue over the nipple and then gently grasped it with her teeth. Lauren placed her hands on Raynee's face, pulling her back to her mouth, kissing her with a furry that had them both moaning and moving their lower bodies in unison.

Lauren, with her hands still on either side of Raynee's face, pulled her head back slightly. Looking into Raynee's eyes, she said, "I want...no, I need to make love to you Raynee."

"Yes," was all Raynee could manage to say.

Raynee pulled herself up, then extended her hand to assist Lauren. Silently, they walked hand in hand to the master bedroom.

As they neared the bedroom, Raynee became more nervous. It had been several years since she had been intimate with a woman. She couldn't get the fact that Lauren was Alex's cousin out of her head. Her heart was racing and she had butterflies going crazy in her stomach. As they crossed the threshold, Lauren dropped her hand and turned to face her. The look in her eyes was all she needed to see to know there was no turning back.

"Are you okay with this?" Lauren asked quietly as she leaned in to nuzzle her neck.

"Ummm...don't talk...just take me to your bed. I don't want to think. I just need to feel your naked body next to mine." She reached down and began pulling Lauren's unbuttoned shirt off. She dropped it on the floor and reached out to touch her breasts. "You are so beautiful," she said as she gazed at the breasts in front of her. Pushing back the lacy bra, she began stroking them. She could feel the nipples harden under her touch. She closed her eyes, taking in the feel of the woman before her.

"You have wonderful hands. Take my bra off so I can feel all of you"

Not one to disobey, Raynee pushed back the bra and allowed it to join the discarded shirt. Her hands immediately went back to Lauren's breasts, kneading them as she caressed the nipples. She reached forward and took one into her mouth and she continued the caress of its sister with one hand. She felt Lauren shiver and wrapped her arms around her body pulling her closer.

Lauren reached over her back and pulled Raynee's shirt up, but was unable to remove it since her mouth was attached to Lauren's breast. Leaning into Raynee's ear she whispered, "Let's get this off so I can see you."

Raynee complied by lifting her arms and removing her mouth from her current favorite place. Before she could dive back in, Lauren reached behind her and unclasped her bra and let it fall to the floor. "Nice," she purred as she pulled Raynee to her, their breasts touching, their lips following suit.

"I don't think I can stand here much longer with you kissing me like that." Raynee pulled back to catch her breath. "You have amazing lips."

Lauren reached down and unzipped Raynee's pants, then held her hand as she stepped out of them. The royal blue thong before her took her breath away. Fingering the edge, she licked her lips. "This is H-O-T." She pushed her finger under the edge and tugged at the band pulling Raynee back towards her, once again capturing her mouth. "You are so beautiful," she whispered as she walked her backwards until she felt Raynee's legs touch the edge of the bed. She leaned into her, pushing them both onto the bed. Lauren's leg landed between Raynee's and she began moving against the silk of the thong.

"Please...get...naked...need...to...feel...you." Raynee could barely express her thoughts with the pressure on her sex blocking her speech.

Lauren pushed herself up and quickly shed her pants and underwear. Before Raynee could sneak a peek, she was back on top of her. Their tongues once again engaged in a dance as they crossed the line from friends to lovers.

◊◊◊

Lauren awoke to the feel of gentle kisses being placed across her back. She reached back and cupped the butt behind her, pulling it closer. "Um...that feels nice."

"Umm, yes it does." Raynee stretched her arm around Lauren, placing her hand on her breast. She gently stoked her nipple feeling it harden under her fingertips. Leaning forward, she began kissing up Lauren's back until she reached her neck where she continued to place gentle kisses. Her own nipples went instantly hard as she pressed against Lauren's back. When she hit the spot she had recently discovered drove Lauren wild, she shifted as her new lover slid onto her back. Lauren reached up with her left hand, placing it on the back of Raynee's head and pulled her to her lips. The kisses increased in intensity as Raynee's hand continued their journey over Lauren's chest. She moved from one breast to the other and then back again. Suddenly she felt a hand take her wrist and slowly move it down. The place it landed was warm and very, very wet. "My, my, Ms. Tyson, aren't you ready and willing this morning," she said teasingly as her hand began a gentle caress.

"Mumm..." was the only reply she heard.

◊◊◊

There were lying in bed after making love for the second time that morning. Both were quiet as they spooned, Lauren in the back with Raynee snuggled close in front of her. Lauren was gently stroking up and down the length of Raynee's body. "So, do you think we could do this again?" she asked very desirously into her ear.

"Are you kidding me?" Raynee exclaimed. She tried to turn to face the woman behind her.

Flabbergasted at the response, Lauren wasn't quite sure how to respond. "But, I thought you enjoyed yourself. I mean you seemed to be. I just thought..."

"You have worn me out lady. I couldn't go again if I tried."

Realization setting in, Lauren chuckled faintly as she leaned forward and kissed Raynee on her shoulder. "Sweetie, I didn't mean right now. I meant again, as in, I'd really like to see you again...very soon."

An embarrassed Raynee pulled the pillow over her head. "Sorry," she said shyly. "I just thought you meant now and I was thinking how can she have the energy after last night and this morning? I suddenly felt very old, like I wasn't going to be able to keep up with you." She pulled the pillow away and turned to look into the beautiful eyes she had come to know. "Of course I want to see you again. Last night and this morning was amazing." She held Lauren's gaze as she reached up and placed a soft kiss on her lips. Pulling back, she stated sadly, "I hate to tell you, but I really need to get up. I have to be at the restaurant in a few hours."

"I understand, although I hate for you to leave. Do you want to take a shower first?" Lauren gazed up and down Raynee's naked body as she spoke.

"You, my dear, are incorrigible," she said as she tapped her index finger on Lauren's nose. "I'll shower at home, where it will be safe. Maybe next time I'll let you bathe me." Jumping out of the bed, she went in search of her clothes.

Lauren propped herself up on the pillow and watched Raynee get dressed.

"If you aren't busy tonight, why don't you come to the restaurant later and have dinner with me?"

"I don't want to get in your way at work."

"Well, I didn't say you wouldn't be a distraction, but you would be a very welcome distraction," she winked as a huge smile crossed her face.

"You are so beautiful." She stood and threw on her shirt from the previous evening. Reaching her hand out to Raynee, "Come on, I'll make coffee and fix you a to-go cup."

◊◊◊

After a lengthy goodbye, Raynee headed to her loft. She arrived home and had to hurriedly shower and get dressed. She wanted to get to the restaurant in time to meet with the staff before the lunch crowd began arriving.

As she showered, she relived the events of the previous evening. It was so unexpected and wonderful. Her mind was flashing from moment to moment. She wondered how the evening would have transpired had Chandler and Alex shown up. She and Lauren were already having a great time before Lauren had received the cancellation call from Alex. They were both so relaxed and enjoying each other's company. They had spent time together since Lauren's arrival, but something felt different since the kiss they had shared the previous week.

Looking through her closet, she was a little more selective about what she would wear tonight. Of course, it had nothing to do with the fact she had a dinner date later.

She grabbed her cell phone as she was walking out the door. Looking down she realized she had a missed call. She stopped dead in her tracks when she saw who the call was from. Her elation suddenly vanished. When she got to her car, she dialed her voicemail number to retrieve the message. "Hi Rayn, it's Payton. Sorry I haven't called you back sooner. I want to apologize for my actions the last time I saw you. Can we have dinner this week? Please call me back. I'd really like to see you." She pressed the disconnect button as she sat in the car staring at the phone.

◊◊◊

The early dinner rush was beginning to dwindle. The second round wouldn't begin for about an hour. The in-between group was coming and going, so the staff was able to take a breath. As she was reviewing the late night special with the chef, Lilly, the maître d' came in to the kitchen. "Raynee, you have someone up front asking for you."

Raynee stopped by her office and checked herself in the

mirror, then did a quick breath spray before heading to the lobby. She stopped and made an audible gasp when she saw Payton standing there chatting with Lilly. She quickly scanned the room for any sight of Lauren. Not seeing her, she slowly walked over to Payton.

Payton seemed to feel Raynee as she approached her. Turning she smiled and reached in to hug her. She quickly pulled back when she felt the cold reception to the embrace.

"Hi Rayn. I hope I didn't catch you at a bad time. I left you a message earlier. When I didn't hear back from you I thought you might be here, so I decided to come down and have dinner."

"I received your message, but I've been busy. Lilly can seat you, but this isn't a good place or time for us to talk." Her irritation was growing. Payton knew how she felt about bringing her personal matters to the shop.

"Can I just speak to you in your office for one minute?" she plead.

"I said I'm busy right now." Her tone was harsh she knew, but she was getting more and more agitated the longer Payton stood there.

"One minute, I promise."

Shaking her head, Raynee turned as she stated adamantly, "One minute." She marched back to her office.

Payton closed the door as she entered the small office. Raynee was only a few feet from her and she reached out to touch her face. Her hand was quickly stopped by the smaller hand.

"Please don't Payton. What do you want?" She was quickly losing her patience.

"I just wanted to see you. I know I was an ass the last time I saw you and I wanted to apologize."

"And you did...in your message."

"Will you have dinner with me tomorrow night?"

"I can't."

"Okay, well maybe later then." Turning, she opened the door. "I love you, Raynee."

Before Raynee could respond, she was gone. Raynee stayed in her office for a few minutes composing herself. Payton had made it obvious several times that she only wanted a friendship. Even after everything they had been through, it had taken some time to adjust to that fact. Now she had developed feelings for someone else. She couldn't let her past feelings for Payton cloud the facts. They would only be friends from this point forward.

◊◊◊

Lauren was coming out of the ladies room when she saw Payton leaving Raynee's office. She couldn't help but overhear the words Payton spoke as she left. She stepped back into the restroom before either of them saw her and tried to compose herself. She paced back and forth replaying last night and this morning with Raynee. She thought back to the day Raynee accompanied her to take a second look at her now home. She had no idea about the history between her realtor and Raynee. She really had no reason to. It was before she moved to Atlanta. She reasoned if there was something going on between Payton and Raynee that Raynee wouldn't have spent last night with her. She hadn't forced herself on Raynee had she? She thought back to the two of them talking throughout the evening, how Raynee seemed so relaxed. She honestly thought the feelings the previous evening were mutual. When she had asked to take Raynee to her bed, she had after all said yes. She had asked her again before they got undressed and she had not shown any hesitancy. No, she was sure Raynee had wanted it as much as she had. Even this morning, she didn't jump up and leave. She had made love to Lauren before she left. Surely she wasn't able to fake something so intimate without Lauren picking up on it. *Okay Tyson, quit acting like a teenager hiding out in the bathroom. Talk to Raynee. You'll know if something is going on with Payton.* With that thought in mind, she composed herself and walked out to let Raynee know she had arrived.

◊◊◊

Megan knocked on the office door and Raynee acknowledged her by yanking open the door. "WHAT DO YOU...Oh Megan, I'm sorry." Embarrassment immediately showed on her face at the realization. "I'm truly sorry. What do you need? I just had an unexpected situation."

"Lilly was busy and asked me to let you know there's a lady up front asking for you." Megan had only been working at the restaurant a few weeks. She was obviously uncomfortable in the presence of the older lady.

"What does she look like?" She demanded. Surely, Payton wouldn't ask to see her again.

"I didn't see her, sorry. Do you want me to tell her you aren't available or something?" she said shifting from one foot to the other.

"Megan. I apologize for being so short with you and putting you in the middle of this. Just tell Lilly I'll be right there."

Megan turned to leave, but was stopped short. "Megan, thank you," she said sincerely then closed the door as the young employee walked away.

Raynee took several deep breaths and tried to get herself together. If it was Payton, then she had to maintain her cool in front of the customers and staff. If it was Lauren, then she needed to not let her see she was upset. She had to get it together and prepare herself for whoever was here to see her.

She checked herself in the mirror again, took another slow deep breath and walked back to the front. A huge smile covered her face at the sight before her. *I would recognize that tushie anywhere.* She walked up behind Lauren and wrapped her arms around her. Lauren turned in her arms and hugged Raynee.

"Hi, you. I missed you." She whispered in Lauren's ear.

"Umm," she said as she inhaled the scent that was totally Raynee. "I sure hope so, because I couldn't wait to see you again."

Stepping out of her embrace, Raynee took Lauren's hand and walked her back to the bar. Patting an empty stool, she said, "Have a seat and let me get us a glass of wine."

"Drinking on the job these days?" Lauren laughed as she spoke.

"Just one with a very beautiful lady," she said as she perused the bottles. "Ah, I know the perfect wine for this evening." She noticed her hand was shaking slightly as she poured the liquid. She was dismayed to see that the tremor didn't go unnoticed by Lauren, who declined to comment.

"This wine is delicious. What kind is it?" She took another sip of the rich red drink.

"I'm glad you like it, it's a Cabernet Franc. This particular one is one of my favorites." She looked at Lauren as she spoke, watching her lips as she unconsciously licked them. Watching her actions was causing Raynee to feel the flutters in her lower region. "You know you really need to stop." She said as she stared at the mouth before her.

"What? Stop doing what?" She feigned innocence, then laughed as she watched the expression on Raynee's face as she continued the action.

After they finished their meal with only a few interruptions from the staff, Raynee stood and took Lauren's hand to help her from the barstool.

"I guess I need to get out of here, you need to get back to work."

"Just a sec, come with me." She held Lauren's hand as she walked to the back of the restaurant. Opening the office door, she held the door to allow Lauren entry. She stepped in and closed the door behind her. Lauren turned at the sound and Raynee pulled her into her arms. She gazed into her eyes for a second before lifting her mouth to Lauren's. The kiss was deep and full of the passion Raynee had felt when watching Lauren while they ate.

"I've wanted to kiss you since I saw you in the lobby. You have no idea how much I needed to see you right now." She held Lauren in her arms as she spoke.

"Hey, you're shivering. Are you okay? Is there something the matter?" She pulled back to look into Raynee's eye as she spoke.

"No, everything's fine now. Thank you so much for having dinner with me."

"Thank you for taking the time to eat with me. The meal was incredible."

The knock on the door interrupted them. Dislodging from Lauren, Raynee opened the door. "What's up Lilly?"

"Can we accommodate a party of 25 in 30 minutes? It's 8:45 and I didn't know if you wanted to open the private room this late."

"Are Jana and Billy still here?" she asked, referring to her two best servers.

"Yes. Do you want me to alert them? I can shift Megan and Beth to take over their stations, if that's okay."

Lilly obviously had things handled; she just needed Raynee's confirmation. After working with her for over five years, she knew the business and knew how Raynee and Sara liked things. She was a huge asset. "It sounds like you have it under control. I'll be out to greet them when they arrive." Wrapping up the plan, she waved her hand towards Lauren. "Lilly, this is Lauren. Lauren, Lilly is our top-notch maître d' and assistant manager. We are lucky to have her."

The ladies shook hands, Lilly looking Lauren up and down. "It's very nice to meet you Lauren. I hope we see you around more often."

Placing her hand on Lauren's back, Raynee interjected, "I'm sure we will," as she kept her gaze on Lauren. "Thanks Lilly," she added, effectively dismissing the younger lady.

Laughing as she closed the door, Raynee just shook her head. "You better watch that one, she likes older women."

"Are you calling me older?" Lauren said, placing her hand on her chest in mock shock.

"Not too old for me, but probably for Lilly." She closed the distance between them and placed a quick kiss on Lauren's lips. "Now I really do need to go so you can prepare for the group coming in. Thanks again for a lovely evening."

"Thank you. I really enjoyed it." Raynee was back in business mode, but took the time to place another quick kiss on Lauren's lips before opening the door and walking her out.

CHAPTER 19

The weeks leading up to Thanksgiving were busy for Raynee. She and Chandler had discussed the menu for Thanksgiving Day and had compiled the shopping list. She was so busy running the necessary errands to ensure a successful weekend she nearly forgot about packing clothes. She and Lauren were planning to leave Wednesday morning while the rest of the group wouldn't arrive until later. Alex had an early afternoon meeting she was unable to reschedule, so Chandler planned to pick her up after her meeting and drive down. Sam and Lexie were having dinner with Lexie's parents, so they wouldn't arrive at the beach until Thursday morning.

Raynee picked up the last of the menu items and headed back to the loft. She was exhausted but still had a lot to do to be ready to leave in the morning. It was nearly 10 p.m. and she still needed to finish packing, grab a bite to eat, and load what she could in the car. Her cell phone rang and she smiled as she answered. "Hi."

"Hi yourself. Are you about ready for Thanksgiving? I am so excited to finally see your beach house."

"I just left the store and am heading home now. I still have a lot to do, but I'll be ready."

"I wish you would let me bring something. Just because I'm not a chef like you and Chandler doesn't mean I couldn't help."

"Not this year. You are my special guest this year. Now next year, you'll be in the kitchen chopping along with Alex."

"Already planning for next year? I like the sound of that."

"Well...I mean...if you want to go next year..." she backpedaled.

"I can't think of anywhere else I would want to be."

Raynee was trying to wind up the conversation as she neared her parking garage. "I'm almost home, so I'll see you..." Just then, she looked at her guest parking spot and saw a familiar car with a gorgeous woman leaning on it. "I better go, there's someone here waiting for me." She said as she disconnected the line and a huge smile crossed her face.

◊◊◊

As she stepped out of her car, Raynee grinned at Lauren. "I was just talking to an incredible woman on the phone."

"Really? Tell me more."

"Well, I was going to invite her over tonight."

"I can leave." She bent her head down, poked out her bottom lip and turned back toward her car.

Raynee reached out and stopped her, then kissed Lauren gently on the lips. "No way am I letting you leave now." She looked Lauren in the eyes. "You goof. I'm glad you called. I needed to see your smiling face."

"I thought you might need some help tonight." Holding up

a bag she continued. "And some dinner."

"You are the best. Thanks for thinking of me." She opened the trunk and grabbed a canvas bag handing it to Lauren. "If you can take this one, I'll get the rest."

They walked into the loft and as soon as the bags were deposited on the counter, Raynee turned and grabbed Lauren, pulling her close. She placed a long kiss on her lips then rested her head on her shoulder and held her tight. "You don't know how happy I am to see you. It's been a busy week and it was especially long since I haven't seen you in five days."

"I know what you mean. With finals and classes winding down, it was busy, but I couldn't wait until tomorrow morning to see you. I hope the bringing you food excuse is okay."

"You don't need an excuse. I missed you. Besides, you can help me load the car tonight. Have you already packed?"

A slight blush colored her face and she turned her eyes to look around the loft. "Well...yes....my bags are sort of in my car."

Raynee threw her head back as she laughed. "So were you planning on going home tonight?"

"Only if the food excuse didn't work," she snickered.

"Go get your things you'll need in the morning while I get our plates ready." She pecked Lauren on the lips and gave her a tap on the behind to send her on her way. Watching Lauren walk to the door, she thought, *Suddenly I don't feel quite as tired.*

◊◊◊

After a quick meal accompanied by a glass of Chardonnay, Raynee started doling out chores for Lauren as she cleaned up the kitchen and gathered items to be packed for the trip. In short order the car was packed and the cooler was out and ready to be packed in the morning.

"That wasn't too bad," Lauren stated as she looked around to ensure her to-do list was completed.

"Thanks to you." She walked up behind Lauren and wrapped her arms around her. "The only thing left is for me to pack."

"Well, packing would be easy if everyone else wasn't coming. You would just need your beautiful birthday suit." She wiggled her eyebrows as she turned and looked back at Raynee.

"While I love that idea, it will have to wait for another time. Besides, I am very excited for you to meet my baby brother. He keeps asking why he hasn't met you yet."

"You would think with both of us at the same university we would have run into each other at some point. If he's anything like his sister..." Lauren turned in Raynee's arms and kissed her as she stroked her back.

"Enough about my brother, come help me pack so you can take me to bed." She grabbed Lauren's hand and led her to the bedroom. Taking her by the upper arms, gently sat her on the edge of the bed. Leaning down, she removed each of her shoes and gently rubbed each foot before putting it back on the floor. "Now slide back against the pillows and relax while I pack."

Raynee pulled out several shirts and held them up one by one as Lauren appraised each of them. "The green looks great on you...and I think the beige too. How about the V-neck black shirt you wore the night we were at Alex and Chan's?" She winked as she licked her lips.

"Do you have a one-track mind?" She laughed as she threw the rejected pink shirt at Lauren.

"Only when it comes to you." She jumped up and kissed her all over her face and neck, sending Raynee into a laughing frenzy. "It's your fault for being so darn adorable."

"Umm...I could hold you forever. You feel so good. Soft in the right places, firm in other places." Her hands traveled up and down the length of Lauren as she spoke.

Patting Raynee on the butt, she said, "Now finish packing so I can get you in bed like you promised me."

"Yes ma'am." She pulled away, but not without one final squeeze to Laurens butt cheeks.

◊◊◊

Even though they went to sleep very late, Raynee was awake bright and early the next morning. She propped up on her elbow and watched Lauren as she slept. Just as she reached out to touch her face, a hand flew up and grabbed her arm. Raynee squealed as Lauren's eyes popped open and she started laughing at the shocked look on Raynee's face.

"You shouldn't mess with a sleeping woman," she said, pulling Raynee down on top of her.

"Well if this is what it gets me, I'll wake you every chance I get." Leaning in she began kissing Lauren. "You have the best lips. They are so soft. I could kiss you all day."

"Right back atcha. Should we stay in bed for awhile?" She looked at her hopefully.

"I thought you were anxious to get to the beach."

"Oh, I am, but you make it really hard to get up."

"Why don't we go ahead and go this morning, then we can have most of the day at the house before Chandler and Alex arrive."

"That sounds like a great plan."

◊◊◊

Raynee brewed a pot of coffee while Lauren showered. She gathered the last-minute items and began packing the cooler. Checking her list once more, she was satisfied she hadn't forgotten anything. Hearing the shower turn off, she poured a cup of coffee and walked into the bathroom. A very naked, very wet Lauren was standing in the oversized open shower bent at the waist, towel drying her hair.

As she straightened up to begin drying her body, she caught the smell of the coffee. Looking up she saw a very happy looking Raynee leaning on the counter holding a steaming cup. "I thought you were going to join me," she said as she frowned at the gorgeous lady in front of her.

"I meant to, but then I started packing the cooler and checking off the items on the list. Sorry, but I brought a present to make it up to you." Placing the coffee on the counter, she reached for the towel. "Let me dry your back."

Lauren handed her the towel and turned to offer her back.

Raynee opened the towel and began blotting the tops of Lauren's shoulders, slowly working her way down her back. As she dried each area, she placed a kiss on the smooth dry skin. After she had dried the length of her back, she knelt and began drying her firm buttocks. Running the plush towel up and down each cheek, she dropped the towel and, taking Lauren's hips in hand, turned her around. Leaning forward, she placed a kiss at the apex of her thighs. Inhaling deeply, she looked at the face looking down at her. "You are so beautiful and you smell yummy, like vanilla sugar."

She stood up and began kissing Lauren with a passion she didn't know she still had. Walking her backwards until her shoulders were against the still warm shower wall, she dropped back to her knees, pulled Lauren's leg over her left shoulder and began to feast.

When Lauren felt she couldn't stand any longer, she slid down to join Raynee on the shower floor. "Um....that was quite an apology for missing the shower. Unfortunately, I'm going to have to join you when you shower, otherwise I'll smell of sex all day."

"I don't mind." Placing a kiss on her cheek, then pulling back she added, "There's nothing wrong with the smell of sex."

Lauren popped her on the arm as she pulled herself up. "You are so funny. Now get those clothes off and I'll help you shower."

"So you really don't want to get to the beach house today, do you?" She allowed herself to be pulled up and stood while Lauren removed her tank top and shorts.

Turning the shower back on, the duo took their time washing each other, careful not to forget any crevice or cranny.

About an hour and a half later, they were in the car, the top down as they headed to the beach house. It was an unusually warm day for this late in November. If this weather held for the next several days, it should be a perfect weekend.

◊◊◊

They arrived just before noon. As they drove down the long drive to the house, Lauren turned her attention from the lady beside her and began taking in the sights and smells of the Atlantic coast. Having grown up in Texas, she had never been to the East Coast beaches before and wasn't sure what to expect. The moss hung low from the huge trees lining the drive and the cool breeze rushed across her face. Suddenly the smell of the salt water invaded her senses. "Can you smell it? It smells so wonderful!"

Just then, they cleared the trees and the house came into view. "Oh my gosh, Raynee. This is beautiful."

Stopping the car in front of the house, she jumped out and ran around to open the door for Lauren. "Come on, I'll give you the nickel tour before we unload the car."

Raynee unlocked the front door and was immediately thankful for the service she hired to maintain the property for her. The house was cool and didn't at all smell like it had been closed up for the past few months. As they walked through the entry into the kitchen, she smiled at the basket of fresh fruit. She plucked the note from in front of it smiling as she read it aloud. "'Welcome home Ms. Waters. Have a wonderful Thanksgiving. Sheila and the staff of Welcome Home.' Welcome Home is the company that takes care of the place when we aren't here. They keep an eye on the place, keep the grounds maintained, and will even clean it before you arrive."

"Cute name for the company."

"They do a great job. If they ever find anything, they alert me right away. They will even prepare the house if a hurricane is headed this way. Thankfully, I haven't had to deal with that yet, but it's nice to know a reputable company has my best interest at heart." Taking Lauren by the hand, she said, "Let me show you around. First of all my favorite part." Raynee opened the full-length glass doors leading to the deck and pool.

After taking a couple of steps onto the deck, Lauren just stood with her mouth open. "How can you stand not being here all of the time?" She looked at Raynee in amazement.

"It's a great place to get away from the city and I do as much as I can, but not as much as I would like. I keep thinking maybe one day I'd like to live here full time." Shrugging her shoulders, she added, "Maybe one day."

Going back into the house, Raynee pointed out the upstairs

loft, guest bedrooms to the left, and the master suite to the right. "Well, that's it. I hope you enjoy yourself and please make yourself completely at home. This is a place for unwinding, relaxing and forgetting about work."

Taking Raynee in her arms, Lauren kissed her. Pulling, she looked deep into her multi-colored eyes. "Thank you for inviting me. I love it here."

"Thanks for coming." Then realizing what she said she felt her face turning red. "Um, I mean..."

Lauren pulled her close and kissed her again, "Well, maybe we can work on that before everyone else arrives." She pulled back and winked at the still blushing Raynee.

◊◊◊

After the tour, they began unpacking the car. Raynee started putting away the food, while Lauren grabbed the last of the bags.

"Where should I put this?" Lauren asked hesitantly pointing to the suitcase in her hand.

Raynee looked up from the open refrigerator door, "In our bedroom," pointing to the door on the right. "That way," she stated matter of factly, then continued the chore at hand.

She missed the smile crossing Lauren's face as she turned to deposit the bags. *I like the sound of that...our bedroom.*

◊◊◊

Once they were settled, they changed into their swimsuits and walked down the beach hand in hand. The sun was warm and the sky was blue with a slight breeze blowing. As far as Raynee was concerned, it was a perfect beach day. Because this was a private beach it was typically not very busy, but with it being a holiday weekend, it was desolate. Raynee loved to walk the beach, especially in the off-season when she could walk a mile either direction without encountering another human.

Taking a deep breath and slowly letting it out, Lauren felt as though everything else in the world didn't matter. Right here right now, it was just her and Raynee. She really liked the thought of that. As they walked, she thought back to how much her life had changed in the past six months. She was in a new city with a new job, a new home, and most importantly, a new girlfriend. When the realization hit her, she stopped in her tracks, jerking the still walking Raynee.

"Are you okay sweetie?" Raynee turned back to look at a rather pale looking Lauren. "What's the matter? Do you feel okay?" She took a step back and placed her hand on Lauren's forehead. "Hey, what happened?"

Lauren was looking down and when she looked up a tear fell down her cheek.

"Hey, what's wrong? Are you sick?"

"No, I'm fine. It just hit me."

"What? Are you in pain?" Raynee was getting concerned.

Reaching out to hold Raynee's face in her hands, she brushed her thumb across her cheeks. "It just hit me how much everything has changed in my life and how happy I am." She looked down again feeling as though she was unable to express what she felt.

"You don't look too happy right now." She placed her fingers under Lauren's chin and pushed upward so they were eye to eye again. "So what's the matter?"

"I just realized...well, I realized..." Raynee's face showed such concern it left Lauren without words.

"Tell me. What is it sweetie?"

The term of endearment sealed it in her heart. "I realized I'm falling in love with you. Please don't say anything. I mean you don't have to say anything..."

Raynee pulled her close, their lips meeting as their bodies merged into one. The heat from the kiss was almost too much for either of them. Pulling away suddenly, gasping for breath, Raynee looked deep into the bluest eyes she had ever seen. "Wow, you sure know how to sweep a woman off her feet." The smile crossed her face felt like her face would split. "I love you, too," she said tenderly.

CHAPTER 20

Chandler and Alex arrived late afternoon. After getting settled in their usual bedroom and changing into their swimsuits, they joined Raynee and Lauren on the deck. Raynee had prepared a pitcher of mojitos and she was sitting on the end of the chaise where Lauren was reclining.

"Hi, you two. It's about time you got here," Lauren greeted her cousin and her partner.

"Grab a couple of glasses from the bar, the mojitos are in the fridge, or there's beer and wine if you would rather." She pointed to the outdoor bar as she spoke.

Chandler headed toward the bar to the right of the pool. "What would you like honey? Those mojitos look pretty good to me."

"That sounds good to me too." Turning to her cousin and Raynee she asked, "So what have you two been up to today, or should I ask?" She chuckled as she took a seat on the end of the chaise opposite them.

The two looked at each other with an intensity that didn't go unnoticed by Alex. Then they replied in unison, "Nothing really."

Chandler handed her a drink and slid in behind her, pulling Alex back to rest on her chest. She raised her glass and said, "Cheers, to a wonderful Thanksgiving weekend."

Everyone joined in raising their glasses and repeated, "Cheers."

"So...what's going on?" Chandler continued. "Hey Lauren, what do you think of Raynee's digs? Pretty nice down here isn't it?"

"It's beautiful. I already told Raynee I didn't know how she could stand to leave here. It's like paradise."

"I'm just glad she is so generous in sharing it with us. It pays to stay on her good side."

"Very funny...and I am sitting right here. You know I consider it your place as much as mine. You guys are family to Sam and me. I can't imagine having this and not being able to share it with friends and family."

"You are such a generous person Raynee." Lauren leaned in and placed a kiss on her lips. "We are all very lucky to have you in our lives."

Raynee blushed as she looked at Chandler and Alex, then quickly back to Lauren. Lauren caught the slight change in color and pulled back. She was a little taken aback at the slight change in Raynee.

Alex caught the subtle shift in Raynee and quickly interjected. "So, is anybody else ready for a refill?"

Lauren jumped up. "I am. I'll get them." She looked down at Raynee, "Would you like one?"

"Yes, please. I'll go in and get some snacks while you two

take care of the drinks."

Alex patted Chandler on the leg and whispered something in her ear, then Chandler got up and headed to the door close behind Raynee, "I'll help you."

When the girls had gone inside, Alex joined Lauren at the bar. "So really, how is everything with you two?"

"Fine. Well, at least I thought we were fine. I'm not sure what just happened."

"Raynee can be very shy at times, even around us. She isn't used to having someone in her life she can be open about. Things were a lot different when she and Payton were together. She always felt like she had to hold back because of the way Chandler felt about Payton. Just be patient with her."

"She doesn't talk about Payton, so I really don't know much about that part of her life. I do know there was a lot of tension between them when Raynee went to look at the house with me the second time. Actually, the tension came from Payton. Before that day, I didn't even know they knew each other. Then I saw Payton at the restaurant a few weeks ago and I overheard her tell Raynee she loved her. I really care about her, Alex. I just don't want to get blindsided by someone else who may or may not still be in the picture."

"You should talk to her about it." She touched Lauren's arm. "She's a complicated little thing sometimes, but she's a great lady. If I didn't think so, I never would have tried to set you up with her." She winked at her cousin.

"Well, you know she isn't the easiest person to get to open up about personal matters."

"I'll talk to her this weekend if you want. I'm sure she is talking to Chandler now. Chandler is her sounding board. I know you two have been out a few times, and Chan and I both think that's great. If she wasn't interested in you, she wouldn't have invited you down here for the weekend. This weekend is extremely special to her." Alex pulled Lauren in for a hug.

Lauren absorbed the information from her cousin. Obviously, Raynee hadn't shared with them how much time she and Raynee had actually been spending together. Everything had happened so fast since the last time the four of them had dinner together and she had walked Raynee to her car. The kiss they shared that night right before they got busted by Chandler and Alex was the beginning of what had seemed to be a rollercoaster romance. She knew she hadn't known Raynee very long, but she knew she had quickly become a very important part of her life. The realization she had earlier had really taken her by surprise, but she wasn't ready to share that information with her cousin. Perhaps she should back off some. The last thing she wanted or needed was a broken heart.

◊◊◊

After dinner, everyone adjourned to the den where they continued catching up from the activities of the past few weeks. Alex sat on one end of the couch and Chandler stretched out with her head in her lap. Raynee and Lauren sat at opposite ends of the opposing couch.

During a lull in the conversation, they heard a noise. Everyone looked in the direction of the long, lean lady stretched out on the couch. They chuckled in unison at the sound of Chandler snoring. Alex rubbed her hand up and down her lover's arm. "Hey sweetie, let's go to bed."

Chandler jumped up sitting on the edge of the couch and groggily replied, "What...what did you say? I wasn't asleep."

Laughter filled the room and Alex stood and took her hand, pulling her up. "I know honey, I'm just tired. Take me to bed."

"Oh, okay, sure, if you're sleepy." They headed for the

bedroom, and Chandler held up her hand, waving at the two remaining ladies. "Night girls. See you in the morning."

Raynee turned to Lauren, who was still smiling. "Are you tired? Do you want to go to bed? Or would you like a late night stroll on the beach?" She reached across the back of the couch and stroked Lauren's arm.

Lauren tilted her head as she gazed at Raynee. So many thoughts flooded her head. How did Raynee get into her head, her mind, and her body so easily? She wasn't one to fall hard and fast. At least she never had before. There was something about Raynee. So kind, generous, caring, and loving, yet so complicated and often closed off from the rest of the world. She truly was a complex, multi-layered lady and Lauren was enjoying pulling back each layer, anxious to discover what lay beneath.

Their fingers entwined as they gazed into each other's eyes. The desire Lauren saw building in Raynee's eyes was almost more than she could stand. Gliding across the length of the couch, she touched her lips to Raynee's soft subtle ones. She was unsure if the spark she felt as they touched was literal or something deep inside herself. She pulled back for an instant, then leaned back in as they wrapped their arms around each other. The kiss was so full of passion, yet so tender. Lauren felt her whole body shiver. *What is this woman doing to me?*

Lauren pulled back. "Um....I don't think I'm the least bit sleepy after that. My whole body feels alive and tingly." She reached up to touch Raynee's face. "What have you done to me?"

Shaking her head, she stood and reached for Lauren's hand. "Come walk with me. It's my favorite time to walk on the beach. I promise not to keep you out too long," she plead.

The pleading was unnecessary; Lauren knew she would do

whatever Raynee wanted her to do.

As they walked down the beach, Raynee took Lauren's hand. "Is this okay? I'm kind of a touchy-feely girl sometimes."

"It's perfect. I love holding your hand. I just love touching you." Giving her hand a little tug, Lauren stopped. "Do you mind if I ask you something?"

"Of course not. What would you like to know?"

"Did it make you uncomfortable when I kissed you in front of Alex and Chandler?"

Raynee looked down, kicking at the sand. "Kissing you doesn't make me uncomfortable. Kissing anyone in front of Chandler bothers me. You have to understand, Chan knows me better than anyone. She has been with me through relationships, the death of my parents, with Sam, through school. She's my best friend. I just don't want her to think this is something it's not."

Lauren pulled her hand back, stinging from the last words.

Raynee looked up at Lauren's face when she pulled her hand away, and must have seen the look of hurt and sadness on her face. "Wait, that didn't come out right. What I meant was, I think we have something very special, but it has happened so quickly. I usually tell Chan everything going on with me. Everyone has been so busy the last several weeks; I haven't had a chance to talk to her. Not to get her approval - don't misunderstand. With everything that has happened with Payton and then you and us, I just didn't want her to think this was some casual thing. Because it's not. I just need to talk to her and let her know how I feel. That's all."

"Raynee, there's something I need to admit..."

Raynee look cautious as she regarded Lauren's face, and

tentatively she said, "Okay, should we sit down?" She pointed to the Adirondack chairs a few steps away.

"Sure," Lauren said as she took a seat.

Raynee sat beside her and turned to face Lauren.

"Remember the first night together, the next morning you asked me to come to Pabulum to have dinner with you."

"Yes," she replied hesitantly.

"When I arrived, I went to the ladies room before I told Lilly to let you know I was there."

"Okay."

"I heard her." Lauren looked up tentatively.

"Who? What? What are you talking about?" Raynee seemed genuinely confused, then her face betrayed a glimmer of recognition. "Do you mean you heard Payton and I talking?"

"Yes, as I stepped out of the ladies room, I heard her tell you she loved you." Lauren looked Raynee in the eyes. She needed to see her eyes when she asked her. "Are you sure it's over between the two of you?"

Raynee reached out and took Lauren's hand. She looked deep into Lauren's eyes. "Oh sweetie, I'm very sure. She came over to try to get me to talk to her and to work things out. But I already knew there wasn't a chance of us getting back together. It couldn't happen, because I already had feelings for you. It's been over two years since she left. The damage was already done, but foolishly I held on to what we had in the beginning. Sometimes it just takes me a while to accept the facts."

Lauren stood and pulled Raynee up and into her arms. She held her tight, wanting to absorb the pain from Raynee into her own body. Suddenly realizing she was holding her a little too tightly, she loosened her hold and felt Raynee relax. Placing her mouth to Raynee's ear, she whispered so faintly, it was barely audible above the sound of the surf. "Always remember, I love you."

◊◊◊

Chandler woke around 8 a.m. anxious to get started on the Thanksgiving festivities. She wanted to have lunch fully underway so she could enjoy at least part of the Macy's Thanksgiving Day parade, a highlight of the day right behind the turkey.

She felt the warm body snuggled closely behind her and squeezed the hand that was draped across her chest. Turning slightly, she kissed Alex on the lips and continued the kisses across her face and down her neck. "Happy Thanksgiving, beautiful. Time to get up."

The indiscernible reply made her chuckle. She continued the kisses, now extending the kisses lower on the warm naked body.

"Um...don't stop." Alex turned on her back and pulled her lover down on top of her.

"Don't tease the animal." Alex knew how much Chandler loved to make love first thing in the morning. "Do you know what all we have to do before the parade begins?"

"You started it honey. I was just trying to give you better access," she said while rubbing her hands down Chandler's naked body to massage her butt.

"Okay, but just a quickie. You know how much I love the parade."

"You are such a romantic." Alex laughed as she pushed her lover down the length of her body. "You better get started."

◊◊◊

After a quick shower, Chandler threw on some shorts and a T-shirt and went to wake the rest of the house while Alex still lay in bed.

"I'll bring you a cup of coffee as soon as it's ready. I'll go wake the girls."

Realizing what she was about to do, Alex tried to stop her, "Chan wait..." It was too late; she was already down the hall.

A few seconds later, she was back. "Alex, what the heck? Lauren isn't in her room. Oh, I guess she left it for Sam and Lexie. She's probably in the loft. Be back in a few with the coffee honey." She was gone again before Alex could respond.

Please don't go in Raynee's room. Alex thought. She had a feeling she knew where Lauren was and wasn't sure how Chandler would react.

Chandler reached the door of Raynee's bedroom, grabbed the doorknob and threw open the door like she had done a thousand times before. What she encountered almost knocked her on her butt.

Raynee was lying on her back with Lauren straddling her face. Lauren's hands were on the headboard and her face thrown back. Raynee's hands were wrapped around Lauren's thighs as she gently held her in place.

Moaning and the sound of sex hit Chandler like a lead balloon. "Oh my God!" she screamed at the same time Lauren screamed the same words with quite a different inflection. Chandler scrambled to find the doorknob that had slipped from her hand. At the same time, Raynee almost bucked Lauren off the bed as she tried to sit up to see who was at the open door.

Lauren flipped off Raynee and quickly attempted to grab

the sheet, which had been thrown to the end of the bed.

Chandler grabbed the door and almost closed it on her foot.

"Chan...stop." Raynee said before she realized what she had said. She really didn't want her friend to stay. Everything had happened so quickly, she didn't understand why Chandler was standing in her bedroom.

Chandler stopped for a second and turned back to catch her friend's eyes only to catch a full frontal shot of both women.

"I mean...go...I...um...just close the door please," Raynee stuttered.

Chandler closed the door and hurried back to the other side of the house.

Chandler rushed to the guestroom, slamming the door as she entered. She tried to speak, but could not find the words. "They were...she was...oh my God...I saw it. My eyes, my eyes!" She dropped on the bed beside Alex and put her head on her wife's chest. "Aurghhhhh."

Alex rubbed her traumatized partner's head in comforting circles. "I tried to stop you." She was laughing so hard her chest was bobbing Chandler's head up and down.

Chandler jerked her head up and looked Alex in the face. "You knew?"

"I suspected."

"Why am I always the last to know?" She shook her head back and forth as she rubbed her forehead.

Alex pulled her in for a kiss. "Honey, they're grown."

"I know, but I saw it happening. That's not part of my best

friend I really wanted to see...or the parts of your cousin I wanted to see."

"But they both have gorgeous bodies. You've seen them in swimsuits. It's not much different."

"Oh honey, what I just witnessed was nothing like two people in a pool. I'm scarred for life. I may never want to have sex again." She held up her index and middle fingers and jabbed at her eyes like she was trying to poke them out. "Make it go away."

Alex pulled the sheet down, exposing her naked body. Moving her hand down her body to the apex of her thighs, she teased, "Then I guess I'll just have to take care of myself from now on."

Chandler slapped at her hand. "Stop it. I'm serious. It was traumatic."

"Baby, come here and I'll help you get the vision of your best friend and my cousin out of your cute little head."

Chandler lay back down beside Alex and let her comfort her until the visions began to dissipate.

◊◊◊

Sam and Lexie arrived as the girls were winding up the preparations for the main meal. They traditionally had a large breakfast, watched the parade, and then had a mid-afternoon lupper, what they called their lunch/dinner combination.

Sam walked in and immediately grabbed Raynee, spun her around and pulled her off the floor as he enveloped her in a hug. Raynee laughed at the antics of her younger, stronger brother.

"Put me down!" She playfully slapped at him then wrapped

her arms around him.

Sam placed her back on the floor and kissed her on the lips. "Hi, big sis."

"Hi, little brother," she returned their usual greeting as she laughed at Sam.

Turning back to the rest of the group. He immediately zeroed in on Lauren. He spread his arms and waved his fingers, urging her in to his open arms.

Lauren smiled as she stepped into his arms.

Sam leaned in as he hugged her and whispered in her ear. "It is so nice to finally meet the woman my sister can't quit talking about."

Lauren returned the hug, then took a small step back. "I'm so glad to finally meet you, Sam."

Sam turned to Lexie and pulled her to his side. "Lexie, I'd like you to meet the famous Lauren." Then turning to Lauren, "Lauren, this is my beautiful Lexie." He beamed as he made the introductions.

Lauren shrugged off Sam's comment as she hugged Lexie and exchanged greetings with her. "Lexie, it's so nice to meet you."

Raynee stood back and admired the man her brother had become. Such a kind, caring young man. She knew right away things had intensified with Lexie. She could tell by the way he kept looking at her. She smiled at the group before her. She felt so lucky to share this weekend here with them.

After hugs were exchanged among the rest of the group, Sam and Lexie retrieved their bags and got settled.

◊◊◊

"It's starting!" Chandler yelled loud enough for everyone in the house to hear as she turned the volume up on the television.

"She's pretty serious about this parade isn't she?" Lexie and Lauren shared a laugh as they settled on the couch, sitting close so they could chat during the parade.

"No talking during the parade. Remember the house rules," Chandler announced.

"Um, Chan...that's not a house rule," Raynee objected.

"Hey, my eyes still hurt...humor me today."

Raynee and Lauren both grabbed the closest pillows and bombarded her at the same time.

"Hey, watch it." Chandler tried to ward off the invasion.

"Now be quiet and watch the parade," Raynee demanded as she laughed and joined Lauren on the couch.

Everyone settled in to watch the beginning of the parade. Every time someone made a comment about a float, a costume or the entertainment, they were warned to "Shhhh..." by an impatient Chandler.

After the first thirty minutes, the parade lost its appeal to everyone but Chandler. Sam and Lexie put on their suits and went to the pool. Lauren joined Raynee in the kitchen, assisting her with tidying up from breakfast and making drinks for everyone.

With Chandler distracted, Alex snuck into the kitchen. Quietly she gathered the occupants and whispered, "So you gave my girl a private show this morning?"

Raynee and Lauren both popped her on the arm as they all burst into laughter.

"Quiet down in there!" Chandler yelled. "Don't think I don't know what you're talking about."

"Oh honey, just relax. You're going to be fine, I promise," Alex continued, trying to console her.

"At least you have good timing Chan," Lauren teased.

"I'm just glad she didn't try to join in." Raynee knew that would get a rise out of her friend. She wasn't disappointed.

"ALEX......make them stop! I'm going to poke my eyes out, then I won't be able to enjoy the parade. Yuck..."

"Okay, okay, they'll behave as long as you use your manners and knock next time."

"I promise there won't BE a next time. Lesson learned!" Chandler proclaimed.

Raynee, Lauren, and Alex all cracked up. They were sure Chandler had learned a lesson today she wouldn't soon forget.

◊◊◊

The next several hours the group spent around the pool and on the beach, with the exception of Chandler who stayed glued to the television until the last float had made its appearance. Alex checked on her periodically to make sure she was okay.

Raynee and Lauren were snuggled up on the chaise together when Sam and Lexie walked back up from the beach. Lexie grabbed the chaise opposite them. Sam stopped at the end of the chair and grabbed his sister's toes. "You look great, sis. I 'm going to blame the huge smile on your face on the beautiful lady you're cuddled up with." He pointedly looked at Lauren. "Thank you for bringing that gorgeous smile back to my wonderful sister's face."

"I told you she's terrific." Raynee looked at Lauren and winked as she spoke.

"Well of course she is. I wouldn't expect any less," he teased her.

Lauren watched the interaction between the siblings. The warmth spreading through her was more than her just being turned on from being so close to Raynee. She was truly overwhelmed at the depth of the relationship she was witnessing between the siblings.

Sam turned to join Lexie, then as if suddenly remembering turned back to his sister. "Hey sis, did you get my message?"

"What message?"

"I called last night to ask you if you were going to make cheesecake. I told you I could pick up any ingredients you might need." Looking hopeful, he added, "So can you? PLEASE?"

"Sorry, I didn't hear the phone ring." She looked at Lauren, "Do you know where I put my phone?"

"I don't remember seeing it since you and I were talking Tuesday night when you got home."

"I haven't needed to call anyone, but I don't remember seeing it. I'll look for it later. I'm sure it's around here somewhere." She immediately dismissed the phone.

"So, can you?" Sam questioned her again.

"Can I what?" Raynee looked up at him like she had no idea what he was talking about.

"Make a cheesecake?" he plead as he looked down at his sister with those sad brown eyes.

"Of course. Anything you want." She chuckled and turned

back to Lauren. "Do you have any special requests?"

Lauren leaned over and whispered something in her ear. Raynee blushed ever so slightly and then leaned in and kissed Lauren.

Sam joined Lexie. "Geez, she's got it bad," he said as he sat down beside her.

"It's nice to see Raynee happy. I really like Lauren. She seems like a nice lady."

"I agree. Raynee can't seem to stop talking about her. I'm glad. She went through a lot with Payton. I'm just glad to see the light back in her eyes."

"So did you tell her yet?"

"No, I thought we could later. Maybe after dinner." He smiled at Lexie, then leaned in and gave her a kiss. "I love you."

"I love you too. Do you think she'll be okay?"

He looked over at his sister and her new love, then back at Lexie. "Yep, she'll be great."

◊◊◊

By mid-afternoon the meal was ready and everyone was ready to dig into the food they had smelled cooking all afternoon. Everyone took directions from Raynee as she called out orders, in a kind way. "Grab that dish, Sam. Lexie will you get the bread out of the oven? Lauren, will you get those two bottles from the wine refrigerator? Alex, help Chandler with the turkey."

Raynee surveyed the table, where everyone was finally seated and ready to eat. She checked off her internal list as she looked - turkey, dressing, vegetables, bread, cranberry coulis - everything appeared to be there. After a second look around, she headed back to the kitchen one final time.

"Hey, grab another serving spoon," Chandler called out.

"Got it. Anything else?" she said as she grabbed a spoon and carving knife from the drawer.

"Yes, hurry up and sit down, I'm starving," Sam plead.

The group laughed at Sam, whom they knew was always ready to eat. He finished pouring the wine as Raynee rejoined them.

Raynee sat and as was their custom, she asked Sam to say the blessing for the meal and for the blessings of the year.

Everyone joined hands as Sam blessed the food, the friendship they shared, the new member of their extended family, and the pending graduation for himself and Lexie.

As they were all ready to dig in, Sam cleared his throat to gain everyone's attention. "Before we eat, I have something to say." He raised his glass and held it up. Everyone collected their glasses and joined him in raising them. After a quick glance at Lexie, he announced, "Lexie, for some strange reason, has agreed to marry me."

Everyone at the table was speechless for a second, then all at once started clinking glasses and shouting congratulations and cheers.

Raynee jumped up from the table and ran to stand behind her brother and future sister-in-law. She grabbed both of them across the shoulders and squeezed. Placing a kiss of the top of both of their heads, she squealed. "Oh Sam, Lexie, I am so happy for both of you!"

Sam looked at Lexie, winked and replied, "I told you she would be okay."

Everyone finally settled down and began to fill their plates. The chatter throughout the meal consisted of how he had proposed, where was the ring, had they decided a date, where did they want to have the ceremony, had they told her parents. Everyone seemed to ask all of the questions at once, but Sam and Lexie were able to answer them one by one and satisfy everyone's curiosity.

As they were finishing the meal, Sam looked over at his sister. "I have one question I need to ask you, sis. Will you be my best woman?"

Raynee almost fell out of her chair. For one of the few times in her life, she was totally speechless. She looked at her younger brother, then around the table at the faces of her friends. A tear ran down her face as she choked out the simple reply. "There's nothing I would love to do more." As she looked up at her brother, she saw a matching tear stream down his face. She leaned over and placed a kiss on his cheek. "I love you so much Sammie." She turned slightly to look Lexie in the eyes. "I love you too, Lexie."

Sam placed his hand on his sister's face. "Raynee, you are one of the most important people in my life. I can't imagine marrying someone you didn't approve of. Thank for you accepting Lexie into our family."

Lauren reached across and placed her hand on Raynee's leg, giving it a slight squeeze. She felt her own eyes swell with tears. When she looked over at Alex and Chandler, they were both wiping tears from their eyes.

Raynee placed her hand on top of Lauren's, feeling comfort in the love she felt radiating from her. As much as she had wanted this to be a special Thanksgiving for Sam, she was overwhelmed with the turn of events. She couldn't imagine it being more perfect.

Raynee refilled everyone's wine glass and they all sat back rubbing their full bellies. As she came back to her seat, she raised her glass. Everyone followed suit. "To my wonderful brother and his amazing fiancée. Thank you for making this the best Thanksgiving ever. And to Lexie, welcome to the family, my little sister."

Sam leaned over and placed a kiss on his fiancée's lips. Turning back to his sister he asked excitedly as he rubbed his hands together, "Now where is my cheesecake?"

◊◊◊

The following morning everyone was seated around the table eating breakfast. Sam took Lexie's hand and looked at his sister. "Sis, Lexie and I were talking last night and well, we were wondering if we could have the wedding here."

"Sammie, you know you can." Raynee beamed as she immediately began thinking of ideas.

Lexie chimed in, "We want to have the actual ceremony on the beach, with just a small group of family and friends. We were thinking maybe we could have the reception out by the pool if that's okay."

"The ceremony will be beautiful on the beach. Of course, you can have the reception here. I'll help in any way I can." Raynee was touched the couple had chosen the beach house for their special day.

Chandler joined in. "I would be honored to help with the food, unless you had something in mind already."

"Chandler, how could we possibly plan our wedding and not consider you making the food? But you and Alex will be our guests too." He looked at Lexie for confirmation before continuing. "We just don't want you so busy with catering that you can't enjoy the party."

"I'll just get someone to manage the crew on the wedding day, but the prep work I'll do myself."

Alex reached over and took Chandler's hand. "I'll help too. It will be our wedding gift to you both."

"No, we'll pay for the catering. That's too much," Lexie protested.

Chandler held up her hand to stop further comment. "It's not negotiable. Please accept this gift. We talked about it last night and it's something we want to do for our little brother and our new sister." She winked as she looked at Sam, then over to Lexie.

In unison, Lexie and Sam both agreed to accept the generous gift. "Thank you."

"Now, what about the guest list and the actual ceremony? Do you know how many people?" Raynee continued. "When did you decide to have the ceremony? We have so much to do."

When she stopped to take a breath, Sam cut her off. "Sis, relax, we have plenty of time. We aren't thinking about having the ceremony until May."

Chandler and Raynee burst out laughing. "Sam, you have no idea how long it takes to plan a wedding." Chandler exclaimed. "My clients usually start planning —one to two years in advance."

Sam and Lexie looked to Raynee for confirmation. Raynee was nodding her head in total agreement to what Chandler was saying.

Lexie looked like a deer in headlights. It was obvious the newly engaged couple had no idea about planning a wedding. Chandler and Raynee exchanged knowing glances and nodded at each other.

"Don't worry about it, we'll take care of the plans," Chandler promised.

Raynee added, "You just give us a list of any specifics and we'll take care of the rest."

Letting out a breath, Sam looked at each of them. "Thanks, guys. You are the best."

They spent the next hour talking about specifics. Chandler and Raynee gave them a list of things they needed to decide together.

While they were chatting, Lauren and Alex cleared the table and cleaned the kitchen. After they had finished their chores, they adjourned to their respective bedrooms, put on their swimsuits, and met by the pool.

Lauren jumped in and swam the length of the pool. When she arrived at the opposite end, Alex was sitting on the edge with her feet in the water.

"So, things seem to be going well with you and Raynee." She looked down at her cousin who was standing in the water.

Lauren squinted as she looked up at Alex. "Yep."

"Yep? That's all I get? Yep?" Alex reached down and splashed water in her cousin's face. "Give me more than yep."

"Yep ma'am? Is that better?" Lauren kicked back with her feet so that she was floating on her back.

"Don't make me come in there after you."

Lauren lifted her head and smiled up at her cousin. She stuck her fingers up and wiggled them in a come-on manner.

Alex stood up and jumped, landing right beside her. The motion knocked Lauren off balance and she began to sink.

When she reached the bottom of the pool, she propelled herself upward and grabbed Alex as she reached the surface. They continued their horseplay, each trying their best to dunk the other.

"What are you two clowns doing?" The shout caught their attention. They both looked up to see Chandler standing beside the pool, hands on her hips. Raynee stood to her left laughing.

"She started it," they both shouted, pointing at each other.

"Well I'm stopping it. You're going to get hurt. Now play like adults or get out," she reprimanded.

Alex swam over the edge and stuck her arm up. "Okay, okay, help me out honey."

Chandler reached down to assist at the same time Alex anchored her foot on the side and pulled as hard and she could, pulling a loudly protesting Chandler into the pool.

"You asked for it now," Chandler shouted as she went after Alex.

Raynee and Lauren looked at each other, both shrugging their shoulders. Raynee grabbed the bottom of her T-shirt and yanked it off it one smooth motion revealing a bikini. She tossed the shirt aside and jumped in.

She swam over to Lauren and wrapped her legs around her waist and her arms around her neck. Lauren leaned in and kissed her as she began swirling them around. They gazed into each other's eyes as they moved away from the horseplay. When they arrived safely in the corner, they began kissing again.

"Ummm, you taste good, like spearmint."

"Well thank you ma'am." Lauren leaned forward and kissed

her again then leaned in and whispered in her ear. "Have I told you today how much I love you?"

Raynee leaned back as much as she could without falling over. She looked thoughtfully at the woman in her arms. "I don't think so," she replied with a grin.

"Well, let me show you then." She kicked off from the side, floating on her back pulling Raynee on top of her. When they were in mid-pool, Lauren twisted so Raynee was on bottom. It happened so quickly that Raynee lost her balance and began to sink. Lauren scooped her up and back into an upright position.

A sputtering Raynee looked at her incredulously. "What did you do that for?"

"I just wanted to make you as wet as you make me." Lauren laughed at the shocked look on her face.

"You are evil." Raynee disconnected herself and went after Lauren, failing in her continuous attempts to dunk her.

After several minutes, the tired couples climbed out of the pool and dropped into the chaise lounges. They were still laughing and discussing who started what when Sam and Lexie joined them.

"You guys act like you're little kids. We could hear you from our bedroom," Sam proclaimed.

"Keeps us young," Chandler announced as she stood and began shaking her head, spraying water on the engaged couple.

"Hey watch it," Sam protested.

"What's the matter? Are you going to melt Sam-I-Am?" Alex inquired.

"Yeah, you guys are too dry." In one swift action, Chandler grabbed him by the hand, propelling both of them into the pool.

Sam popped up from the pool shaking his head on Chandler. "Watch it or I'll sic Raynee Skye on you!"

Lexie turned to run, but was caught by Alex and promptly deposited into the pool. Not wanting to be left out, Raynee and Lauren looked at each other, nodded towards the pool, then jumped back in.

Amidst the jumping around and splashing, someone suggested a game of keep-away. They divided into two groups, couples against each other. Sam jumped out and grabbed the ball, thus beginning the rowdy competition.

◊◊◊

When everyone was tuckered out, they all climbed from the pool. Raynee grabbed a stack of towels from the storage behind the bar and passed them around. Everyone quickly dried off as best they could. Each couple seemed to have self-assigned seating. Chandler and Alex selected a chaise, with Alex sitting between Chandler's legs, leaning casually against her chest. Sam and Lexie sat side by side on the loveseat, while Raynee and Lauren snagged the other oversized chaise sitting side by side holding hands.

"We kicked your butts again," Sam exclaimed, pointing toward Chandler and Rayne. "You must be getting old."

Chandler glared at him. "I got your old," she muttered as she started towards him, Alex grabbed her around the waist and pulled her back.

"Easy sweetie, you might hurt something."

"Oh, so now you are taking HIS side?"

Chandler tried her best to bow up, but failed when the entire group started laughing at her. "You're on - next year. You've got plenty of time to practice." She turned to Lexie and

Raynee. "And Lexie and Raynee Skye, you better get in shape too. We are taking them next year."

Lauren turned to Raynee with a puzzled look on her face. "Raynee Skye? Is that really your name?"

"Raynee Skye Waters!" Alex, Chandler, and Sam all shouted at the same time.

Raynee's face turned red. She looked around and the group, then turned back to Lauren. Shrugging, she explained, "What can I say, my parents were creative."

"I'll say," Sam shouted. "But it's better than what you did to me!"

Lauren looked from Sam then back to Raynee. "What did you do to Sam?"

"Well I was kind of into Dr. Seuss when he was born, and was not too thrilled about a new sibling, so Mom and Dad let me name him. His legal name is Sam Iam. As in Sam-I-Am from the book *Green Eggs and Ham*."

Lauren stared at Raynee for a while, unsure what to say. Finally she exclaimed, "REALLY? And they let you do that to him? Oh, poor Sam."

"Well it does make for a good story," Raynee protested.

"I've gotten adjusted. I don't tell many people. You have to be part of the family to be privy to that information, so mum's the word." He smiled and winked at Lauren.

◊◊◊

All too soon, the holiday weekend was over and everyone was packing their cars for the dreaded drive back to reality.

Sam and Lexie were the first to leave. They promised to

complete their homework which consisted of a guest list and determining a theme and colors for the ceremony and reception. They planned to meet with Chandler and Raynee within the next couple of weeks to continue the planning process.

"What can we help you do Rayn?" Chandler asked as she watched Raynee packing up the last of the food from the refrigerator.

"That's the last of the food. I think that takes care of everything. You guys can go ahead if you want. We'll be out of here in a few minutes." Raynee closed the refrigerator door and walked over to Chandler. She wrapped her arms around her friend. "Thanks for coming and for all of your help. It was a great weekend." She stepped back and looked into her friend's eyes, "Can you believe he's getting married? I am so happy for them."

"I know. It seems like it was just yesterday he was starting college. Now he's about to graduate and get married." She beamed as she spoke. Sam was the closest thing she had to a brother. "Our boy has grown into a man."

They hugged again. As they released this time, Chandler looked at Raynee and closely watched her face as she asked, "So things are good with you and Lauren?" There was concern on her face.

Raynee thought for a second before she responded, "Yes, things are really good, Chan. I'm very happy with her."

"You know I love you and I just want you to be happy."

"I know and I love you too. It's good. She's an amazing woman and she makes me very happy."

"That's good enough for me then." She turned to find her partner, then turned back and kissed Raynee on the cheek. "Be safe and be good. I'll see you in a few days."

"You know I will."

Lauren and Alex were standing by the car chatting when they walked outside. Chandler walked up behind Lauren and wrapped her arms around her. She leaned in to her ear and whispered, "You take good care of my girl, you hear me."

Lauren turned to look Chandler in the face. "Or...?" she questioned.

"Or I'll sic Alex on you," she replied with a grin.

"Um, leave me out of this," Alex protested.

Lauren walked over and wrapped her arms around Raynee. "She's in good hands, I promise."

There were hugs all around and ten minutes of repeated goodbyes before they were finally in the car and driving off. Hand in hand, Raynee and Lauren walked back into the house.

"I hate to leave. This has been a wonderful weekend," Lauren said sadly.

"I'm so glad you were here to share in such a special weekend. Here I was trying to make it so special for Sam, and he and Lexie stole the show with their big announcement. It was perfect. Thank you for being here." She pulled Lauren close as their lips met.

"You have the sweetest lips. But, if you want to get on the road anytime soon, you better keep them to yourself."

"Um...I know what you mean. I don't want to get all worked up and then not be able to touch you during the drive back." Raynee pulled away from Lauren. She suddenly felt very shy. "You know you can spend the night if you want."

"As tempting as it sounds, I really need to get back to my house tonight. I have a whole list of things to get done tomorrow. Final exams start next week and I'm not totally prepared. But how about dinner Tuesday night?"

"That sounds good. I'll check with Sara to see what's going on at the restaurant this week and let you know for sure."

After one last walk through the house to ensure everything was locked up, they headed back to the city.

CHAPTER 21

It was almost 6 p.m. when Payton arrived back at the realty office. She was surprised to see her Aunt Janice's car still in the parking lot. She ran up the stairs and wrapped her hand around the doorknob, expecting it to be locked. It wasn't, so she called out her aunt's name as she walked in, not wanting to startle her. Receiving no reply, she began searching from room to room, calling her name as she went.

The scream that emanated from her was primal – like that of a wounded animal. She fell to the floor and grabbed Janice's hand. It was cold. She touched her face and gently spoke to her. "Please Aunt J, please wake up. Can you hear me? Please wake up."

Scrambling to extract her cellphone from her pocket, she blindly dialed 911 through the tears flowing down her face. Her mind wasn't working and she couldn't remember the address of the office when prompted for the location by the 911 operator. She kept repeating the same line over and over again. "Please don't leave me…not you too. Please don't leave me…not you too."

It seemed like hours before she heard the EMTs and felt

the hands of the paramedic gently pull her away. They immediately began working on her aunt. Taking vital signs, appearing to help her, but all Payton could think about was it wasn't enough. How could she live without Aunt Janice? She was the only family she had left. The only person she could count on. The only one who truly loved her and understood her.

The paramedics loaded Aunt J on the stretcher and turned back to Payton. "We are taking her to Grady. Do you want to ride with us or are you okay to follow in your own car?"

She looked up to see the compassionate face of the man who had tried to comfort her before.

"I'll follow you," but she wasn't even sure if she would be able to hold it together long enough to make it to the hospital. "Is she going to be okay?"

"We have to get her to the hospital now, but we are doing everything we can." The grim look on his face told her otherwise.

Payton nodded her head and followed them out the door. She stood at the ambulance door as they lifted the gurney into the vehicle. Aunt J's face was pale and covered with an oxygen mask. She hadn't moved since Payton found her lying on the floor.

◊◊◊

Speeding through traffic to keep up with the ambulance, Payton grabbed her cell phone from her belt and selected the familiar speed dial number. After four rings, she heard the familiar voice asking her to leave a message at the tone. At the tone, the only words that came were, "Rayn, I'm....I'm on the way to Grady, it's Aunt J..... I can't lose her. Rayn, please I need you." She disconnected the line as she pulled into the emergency room parking lot. The paramedics were wheeling Aunt J into the hospital. She ran to catch up with them, but was quickly stopped by a nurse when she attempted to follow them into Room C.

"I have to go back with her, she's all I have," she begged, tears streaming down her face.

"I understand, but I need for you to give me some information while the doctors work on her." She gently took Payton by the arm and guided her to the small cubicle that was her office. "Can I get you something to drink, coffee or water?"

"No, thank you," she choked out, tears streaming down her face.

The kind nurse, Alice, according to her nametag, gave her a sympathetic look and explained she needed to get some basic information on the patient. She began asking questions while Payton continually turned back to follow any activity coming and going through Door C. She answered as many questions as she could, but was barely able to hold it together. A million thoughts running through her mind, she was unable to focus. *Please be okay Aunt Janice...please.* She placed her elbows on the edge of the desk and lowered her head into her hands.

Alice reached across the desk, touching Payton's hand that was rubbing her forehead. Payton looked up at her as Alice explained she had all of the information she needed for now. "She has a great team working on her. I'm sure they are doing everything they can. Is there someone I can call to sit with you while you wait?"

"No. She's my only remaining family." The terror was evident in her shaking voice. "I don't know what I will do if I lose her." She closed her eyes and the tears began flowing once again.

"Look, my shift is just ending. Why don't I come and sit with you for a while. Is that okay?"

Payton looked up and saw the kindness expressed in the eyes of Alice. "You are very kind. Thank you, I would appreciate it."

◊◊◊

Luckily, the family waiting room was empty except for a couple waiting on news about their daughter who was brought in for pains in her side.

Payton and Alice sat on the opposite side of the room in the firm straight back chairs. Alice had gotten both of them a cup of hot coffee from the employee lounge. Payton held the steaming cup with trembling hands while Alice attempted to engage her in conversation.

"Are you from Atlanta?"

Understanding the motive and appreciating the distraction, she replied. "Yes, I am a native Atlantian, which is rare. I was actually born in this hospital."

"I moved here from Northern Virginia last year. I really like it here. The weather is so much better than up there, and the people are really nice."

"Southerners get a bad rap, in my opinion. We aren't all toothless and go around spitting tobacco."

"No, you appear to have most of your teeth," Alice said as she smiled and winked at Payton.

"Thank you for sitting with me and for the coffee." The conversation helped to calm her down some and the tears were beginning to dry up. She glanced at her wrist and then realized she must have left her watch at home. "I wonder what's keeping the Doctor." She looked around the sterile waiting room at the dull white walls and located a wall clock. It was nearly 8:30. Only two and a half hours since she had found her aunt, but it seemed like much longer.

Hearing a sound at the door she, Alice, and the other couple looked up at the same time, all anxious to receive an update on their family member. The middle-aged doctor walked in. "Janice Ellis's family?" he inquired as he looked around the room.

Payton jumped up. "I'm Payton Mills, her niece and next of kin."

He approached her and gestured to the chair beside Alice. "Please have a seat. I'm Dr. Richard Bryant. Your aunt suffered a severe heart attack. We did everything we could for her..."

Payton's face turned ashen and her hands began to shake. "Please, no...no."

"I'm sorry Ms. Mills, but we were unable to save your aunt."

She latched onto the doctor's jacket, pleading with him. "No, no, no, no...she can't be gone. She's all I have...please be wrong...try again, try harder. There has to be something you can do. Please no, don't let me lose her too. I have money. I'll pay whatever it costs. Give her the best care available. Call whomever you need to. Please...please just don't let her die."

She felt the hand on her back and sharply turned to see tears flowing down Alice's face, her hand rubbing delicate circles on Payton's back. "Can't you make them do something...anything. Please tell them I can't lose her...please Alice..." she begged.

Alice reached over and pulled Payton to her shoulder, and she wept with her.

The two strangers sat their holding each other, one from a loss so severe her heart felt as though it was ripped from her chest, the other trying to ease the pain of a total stranger.

Dr. Bryant rose from the chair beside her and compassionately said, "I am so sorry for your loss. Please know that we did everything we could to save her." He turned and walked out the door, enclosing the pain in the stark waiting room.

◊◊◊

Payton wasn't sure how she arrived home. Her head was spinning with the activity of the past few hours. Dazed, she walked to the kitchen and poured a glass of single malt scotch. She turned it up and emptied the glass. She grabbed the bottle to pour another, but her hands began shaking so badly she almost dropped the bottle. She slid down to the floor, placed her head on her bent knees, and wept.

She wasn't sure how long she slept, but when she awoke, it was still dark outside. She pulled herself up and walked to her bedroom. She laid across the bed and cried herself back to sleep.

It was getting dark outside and she was getting hungry. She ran in to the house and called for Mommie. She didn't get a reply, so she went to the kitchen and got a cookie and a juice pack from the refrigerator. She took it back outside and sat on the steps with Mr. B. She told him about her day at school and about how excited she was to be invited to Ashley's birthday party next week. She explained to him about not all of the kids being invited to the party and how she didn't think that was fair. Mr. B understood about her leaving him at home this year, because he knew she was a big girl now and how important it was to attend first grade. Mr. B was her best friend, but she had to be careful talking about her new school friends, because he got jealous sometimes and wouldn't talk to her.

She finished her juice and cookie and was starting to get

cold, so she went back in the house and called for Mommie again. When she didn't hear Mommie call her back, she started walking through the house, Mr. B clinging snugly to her side. She went to the living room, no Mommie. Her small feet made little noise as she ran down the hallway. The door to Mommie's room was closed. She knocked softly, because that's what you were supposed to do. Mommie said so. She called again "Mommie, Mommie, where are you?" When Mommie didn't reply, she reached up and turned the doorknob. She pushed the door open slowly. She must be tired, she thought, Mommie was taking a nap. She ran to the bed and climbed up beside Mommie, who was facing the window. She gently tugged on her arm, but Mommie didn't move. She climbed over her and fell into the wetness. She raised her hand and saw it was covered in blood. The scream tore through her small body.

CHAPTER 22

After Raynee and Lauren had unpacked the car, Lauren reluctantly left to go home. Raynee felt very lonely. She had loved spending the past few days around her chosen family, and especially with Lauren. Reflecting on the course their relationship had taken in the past few days, she beamed. Pouring herself a glass of wine, she began the chore of doing laundry and putting away the supplies from the weekend.

Raynee wondered around the house, starting one project and then another. The suitcase was unpacked, the unworn clothing was put in the dresser, the first load was in the washer, and the food put away. She grabbed the dirty clothes from her bedroom, including what she had worn last Wednesday. As she was tossing them in the laundry basket, her cell phone fell from the pocket of her khakis. *So there you are. I have to admit I didn't miss you a bit.* She picked up the phone and checked the display. Of course, the battery was dead. She walked back to the kitchen and placed it on the charging station. Finally feeling caught up, she grabbed her glass of wine, plopped down on the couch, and reached for the remote.

She surfed the channels for a while, not finding anything to capture her attention. She finally settled on a sappy movie on

Lifetime and sat back to enjoy her wine. Try as she may, she couldn't get her mind off Lauren. She really wanted to call her and ask her to come back over, but she knew that wasn't fair. Lauren has responsibilities too. It was almost 10 p.m. when she gave up on the movie, turned the television off, and headed to bed.

◊◊◊

After a great night's sleep, Raynee awoke feeling refreshed and ready to start the day. She got up early, worked out in the gym, then showered. She wanted to get to the restaurant early today. There was much to do to prepare for the upcoming week.

As she grabbed her cup of coffee, she remembered her phone, still in the charger. She snagged it and checked the display. It was turned off. *Oops, forgot to turn it back on last night.* She turned it on, dropped it in her pocket and grabbed her keys as she headed to the door.

The beeps coming from her pocket indicated she had messages. Once she cranked her car with the Bluetooth enabled, she connected to her voicemail. She sat with her mouth opened when the automated system announced she had twelve messages. When she heard the voice on the first message, she put the car back in park.

"Rayn, I'm...I'm on the way to Grady, it's Aunt J...I can't lose her. Rayn, please I need you." Beep. The second message was hardly discernible. "Rayn, she's....she's gone." Beep. "Rayn, I need you. What am I going to do?" Beep. "Raynee, please help me." Beep. "Rayn, Ish neesh ya...." beep. The following message was only crying. And so the messages continued, each decreasing in intelligibility.

Raynee disconnected the call and sat in her parking garage for several minutes trying to collect herself. *What had happened? Payton was a wreck and had obviously been drinking.* She threw the car in drive and raced to Payton's house.

When she arrived, the house was dark, but Payton's car was in the drive. She knocked on the door, but no one answered. The windows were frosted, so she was unable to see in the side windows. She raced to the back door and found Payton sitting in the lounge chair. She appeared to be asleep, but when Raynee approached her, she opened her eyes.

"You came." She let out a loud sign as tears ran down her cheeks.

"I was out of town and just received your messages. What happened?" She sat on the edge of the chaise with Payton and placed a hand on her extended leg. The smell of alcohol seeped through Payton's pores and almost took her breath away.

Payton welcomed the heat from Raynee's touch. She leaned up, grabbing Raynee and squeezing her. The tears immediately soaked Raynee's shoulder.

Raynee wrapped her arms around the shaking body next to her. She held her and whispered words meant to comfort, but she knew they went undetected, overshadowed by the deep wails emanating from the inconsolable Payton.

When Payton began to settle down, Raynee placed her hands on her shoulders and pushed her back slightly so she could see her face.

"Can you tell me what happened?" she said delicately. She wiped the tears from Payton's cheek as she spoke.

"I found her on the floor in her office. I don't know how long she had been there. The doctor said she had a heart attack. They tried to save her, but it was too late. She...she died at the hospital."

"When did it happen?"

"Wednesday," Payton choked out.

"Oh honey, I'm so sorry. I left my phone here and didn't receive your messages. Have you been alone the whole weekend?"

"I've...I've been here. I didn't...didn't know what to do. I couldn't find you."

"What about a service?"

"No, she didn't want one. She just...just wanted to be cremated." She pulled up the edge of her T-shirt and wiped her face. "She was all I had and now she's gone." The final comment started the barrage of tears again.

"I know, she was a wonderful lady. I'm so sorry Payton. What can I do?" She pulled Payton to her and gently stroked her back as she spoke.

"Just be here," she choked out.

"I'm here." She sat there consoling her friend until she was able to regain her composure. Only then did she notice the empty bottles scattered on the ground beside the lounge chair.

Raynee pulled back and looked into Payton's eyes. It was obvious she hadn't been sleeping. "When did you last eat?"

"I don't know."

"Okay, I'm going to go in and make you something to eat. But first, let's get you into the shower." Standing, she offered her hand to a shaky Payton.

Leading her into the master suite, Raynee started the shower, pulled out a fresh towel, and instructed Payton to shower while she headed to the kitchen. She took a quick survey of the refrigerator, not seeing much to work with. Checking the expiration date on the eggs, she collected a couple, butter, and cheese.

When Payton emerged from the bedroom, smelling and looking better, she sat her down to a cheese omelet and toast. "Sorry, but your pantry isn't very well stocked." Pouring a cup of coffee, she placed it in front of her. "Now eat up," she commanded.

"Thank you Rayn. I'm so glad you're here." She looked up, the tears threatening to spill over again. "I don't know what I'm going to do."

"Just eat, we'll figure it out." Raynee suddenly remembered she was supposed to be at the restaurant. "Hey, I need to make a quick call. I'll be right back." Stepping out on the patio, Raynee pulled the door closed behind her and walked away from the house as she dialed. Sara picked up on the third ring. "Hey, it's me."

"Hi Raynee, what's up?"

"Um, short version is Payton's Aunt Janice died last Wednesday. I just found out a little while ago and I'm at her house right now. She's a wreck. I hate to leave her alone."

"It's okay, I've got the restaurant. Don't worry about that. But what about her family?"

"Her aunt was her last living relative. She's all alone now."

"Oh gosh Raynee, I'm so sad for her. Is there anything I can do?"

"No, I'm just concerned about her. It appears she's not been eating, but has been drinking quite a bit of scotch among other things. There are empty bottles everywhere." Raynee had found empty bottles in both the bedroom and the kitchen.

"Just let me know if you need anything. And give her our condolences, please."

"Will do, thanks Sara. I'll check in with you later. Bye." She disconnected the phone and looked around. *Oh Payton, I wish I could take away your pain.*

When she walked back in the house, Payton was still sitting at the bar, but her head was on her arm, which was lying on the counter. Raynee walked over to her and gently shook her, waking her. "Come on, let's get you into bed. Then, I'm going to go get some groceries."

"Please don't leave me," Payton plead.

"I'll be right back. Come on, you'll feel better if you take a nap."

"Will you lie beside me, please?"

Raynee hesitated, but the look she was getting from Payton was too intense for her to refuse. "Okay, but only until you go to sleep."

"Okay." Payton extended her hand, which Raynee took as they walked back to the bedroom.

Raynee changed the sheets while Payton brushed her teeth. She walked back into the bedroom just as Raynee was finishing. Raynee tossed the pillow back on the bed and pulled the sheet back. "Hop in."

Payton complied and then slid over making room for Raynee.

Raynee removed her shoes and slipped under the covers. Payton immediately cuddled up against her and placed a kiss on her cheek. Sleepily she murmured, "Thank you, sweetheart." Within seconds, she was fast asleep.

Raynee lay there trying her best to be still so as not to wake Payton. She made a mental list of what to pick up at the grocery store. After what she felt was adequate time for Payton to fall into a deep enough sleep, she started to slide out of the bed. As soon as she moved, Payton moved, sliding her leg on top of Raynee and moving her head to Raynee's chest.

Oh, great. Now what am I going to do? She waited about ten more minutes, silently singing songs to keep from squirming around and waking Payton. When she thought it might be safe again, she extracted herself from underneath Payton. She was successful this time. Grabbing her shoes, she tiptoed to the living room.

◊◊◊

When Raynee arrived back at the house, Payton was still hard asleep. She quietly put away the groceries and started picking up the bottles, which were scattered everywhere. If Payton had consumed all of this, she was drinking practically nonstop for the past four days.

After tidying up and taking out the garbage, she picked up her phone to call Lauren, then remembered she was back in class today. She didn't want to explain why she was at Payton's in a voicemail, so she decided to call her later. She walked back in to the house and heard a scream rip through the house. She took off running to the bedroom, scooped up the screaming Payton and held her tight.

Raynee held Payton until the tears dried up and she stopped shaking. When she finally settled down, Raynee asked understandingly, "Do you want to talk about it?" She had spent many nights comforting Payton from the nightmares that invaded her sleep.

"This time it was Aunt J, instead of Mom. She was in the office, but she was covered with blood." She shivered as she spoke. "Her eyes were open and she was staring at me. Her hand was out and she was screaming for me to help her."

Raynee considered what she had been thinking about while Payton was sleeping and decided she should broach the subject. "Payton, do you think maybe you should speak with your doctor and perhaps she can give you something to help you while you deal with this?"

"No, absolutely not, I don't want to take anything." She was adamant.

"Payton, I um...I noticed you had, well you had a lot of empty bottles all around the house. Honey, you can't drink this away. I'm concerned about you and I want to help you," Raynee plead.

"I'll be okay. I'll quit drinking. Now that you're here, it will be better." She reached up and hugged Raynee, then leaned over and kissed her on the lips.

Raynee was taken aback and tried to stop the kiss. She gently placed her hand on Payton's shoulder and pushed her back. "Wait, Payton."

Looking deeply into Raynee's eyes, Payton reached up and stroked her face. "I'm sorry. I really appreciate everything you have done for me."

Raynee stood and turned back to Payton. "Come on, I stopped by the restaurant and got your favorite soup and a loaf of bread fresh from the oven. Do you think you can eat something now?"

The smell hit Payton as she approached the kitchen. Her stomach growled audibly. "I'll say yes after smelling it," she said as she rubbed her stomach.

Payton sat at the bar again while Raynee filled the soup

bowl and placed the warm bread on a plate in front of her.

"This is delicious," she said between spoonful's of the chicken stew. "Thanks again Rayn, I really appreciate it."

After she finished eating, they moved in the living room. Raynee sat at one end of the couch and Payton sat at the other end. They turned to face each other.

Raynee again tried to talk to Payton about speaking to a professional, but Payton wanted no part of it. She decided she would let it go for now. She was deeply concerned about the excessive drinking given Payton's addictive personality, but she knew that as much as she wanted to help, it was Payton's decision and she could only be there to support her, not to force her.

They sat in silence, each consumed in their own thoughts, Raynee thinking about what Payton had worked so hard to overcome with the drug addiction and how much it had changed both of their lives. She knew they both had changed quite a bit. It had taken her a long time, but she was happy with her life now. She just wished Payton could find happiness...and not in a bottle.

◊◊◊

The vibration in Raynee's pocket startled her. She realized both of them had fallen asleep and somehow Payton's head was in her lap. She reached for her phone, but couldn't get to it without disturbing the sleeping Payton. It eventually went to voicemail and the short vibration let her know the caller had let a voicemail.

Payton suddenly began thrashing around in her lap. "No, no!" she shouted as she kicked her legs about.

Raynee reached down to stroke her face in an effort to gently wake her. When she touched her face, Payton swung her arm at the touch and her closed fist landed on Raynee's lips. Raynee wrenched at the pain, and looked down to see the red blood dripping down on the now waking Payton.

Raynee grabbed her mouth, catching the blood in her hand as Payton, realizing what had happened, tried to sit up. She reached out to touch the bleeding lips.

"Let me up, I need to get to the bathroom." She shoved Payton's hand away and she jumped up and ran to the bathroom.

Payton followed her, shouting, "I'm sorry Rayn. I didn't mean to hurt you. I'm so sorry. Please let me help."

Raynee surveyed the injury as best she could. Applying pressure was not decreasing the bleeding.

"Can you get me some ice and a paper towel please?" She spoke around the tissue she held to her lip.

In a flash Payton was back with the ice. Raynee applied it to her lip and sat on the closed toilet seat. When she could no longer feel her lips, she removed the compress. The split lip had stopped bleeding, but was extremely swollen.

Payton reached out to touch her face, but Raynee pushed her hand away. "Don't touch it, I don't want it to start up again."

"Rayn, I'm so sorry..."

"It's okay. I know you didn't mean to. It will be fine." Raynee looked her directly in the eyes. As she spoke, she reached out and stroked her arm.

Tears flowed down Payton's face as she nodded her head ever so slightly. "You need to stop talking, it's starting to bleed again." She took the ice pack and placed to back on the injury.

Raynee reached out to take over holding the ice. "I've got

it."

Payton stuck her hand out and took Raynee's free hand. "Let's go back to the living room and get you comfortable." She pulled Raynee up, leading her to the other room.

Once she had Raynee settled back on the couch with her feet up, Payton turned on the television and found an old movie that had just started. They settled back and watched, Payton keeping an eye on her the whole time.

When the movie was over, Raynee looked out, realizing it was dark already. Getting up, she announced, "I need to get home. I didn't realize how late it was."

The disappointment showed all over Payton's face. "Can't you stay a little while longer? I can fix us something to eat."

"I really should go, if you think you will be okay alone." She felt bad leaving Payton alone, but knew eventually she would have to go. Perhaps now that she had some sleep and a couple of good meals, she would be in better shape mentally and would stay away from the alcohol.

"Sure, I'll be fine. You should go. I know you have better things to do than stay here." Her tone held the slightest hint of bitterness.

"Payton, I'm sorry. I'm glad I was able to spend the day with you today, but I do have some things I need to attend to. I'll call you later. Okay?"

"Okay." Payton crossed the distance between them and pulled Raynee in for a hug. She held her tight, like she never wanted to let her go. When Raynee tried to pull away, she turned her head and placed her lips against Raynee's.

As soon as she applied pressure, Raynee let out a yelp and pulled back, placing her hand over her injured lip. She felt the blood trickling down her lip as she ran to grab a paper towel.

"Damn, Raynee, I'm sorry. I forgot...I'm sorry" She ran over to Raynee and began rubbing her back. "I didn't mean...I'm sorry." She took her by the shoulders and turned her so they were facing. Looking into her eyes, she tried to express what she was feeling yet unable to verbalize.

"Payton, really it's okay. Now stop apologizing." She knew that look; she had seen is too many times. She had to let Payton know she was there for her, as a friend. She didn't feel it was a good time to discuss her relationship with Lauren, but eventually she had to let Payton know there was someone special in her life. "Now, promise me you will eat something."

"I promise."

"And Payton, please take it easy on the drinking. I worry about you."

"I will. Thank you for coming over and for everything you did. I really appreciate it."

Raynee grabbed her keys from the counter and walked to the back door. As she opened the door, she turned back to look at Payton. "I'll check on you later." She turned and walked out the door, missing the tears flowing down Payton's face.

CHAPTER 23

"Ouch!" Raynee exclaimed as she placed her fingers over her lip. Obviously, the wound reopened during the night, apparent from the blood on her pillow.

Swinging her legs over the edge of the bed, she sat up and placed her elbows on her knees and hands on her face. She shook her head slowly and she replayed the previous day. She hadn't returned Lauren's call and wasn't sure how she was going to explain yesterday. The split lip was truly an accident, but would Lauren understand why she felt she needed to take care of Payton? Her thoughts drifted back to Payton. She was so upset she had turned to the bottle to ease her pain. After all she had been through and the hard work she had put into her recovery, this was not a smart decision on her part. Raynee knew she couldn't fix Payton this time, just like she couldn't fix her before. All she could do was be her friend and be there for her.

Reluctantly, she got up and began her day. She would call Payton later to check on her.

◊◊◊

Sara looked up from the desk as Raynee walked in and

plopped down in the side chair. "What in the world happened to you? Did you get into a bar fight? What does the other guy look like?"

"It's fine, just a little cut." She attempted to blow it off. "Sorry about bailing on you yesterday. Thanks for covering for me."

"How is Payton? Did you get rid of the bottles or were they already all empty?" Raynee had given her the details of Payton and the condition of the house when she had stopped by to pick up the soup yesterday.

"She's a mess. She did sleep some yesterday, but every time I walked out of the room, she would call me back and start crying again. I did get her to eat something. I'm really worried about her, Sara."

"I understand, but you can't fix her, Raynee. Maybe she should talk to a professional." Sara knew too much about their previous relationship and the impact it had on Raynee. Payton had a way of manipulating Raynee, and she didn't want to see her friend go through that agony again.

"I tried to talk with her about seeing a professional yesterday. Hopefully she'll at least think about it." Raynee blew out a loud sigh. "So, what's the special for the day?" She was tired of thinking about the situation with Payton. The best way to get it out of her head was to delve into her work.

Before they both realized it, the lunch rush had passed and they were ready to take a break before the evening rush began.

"I need to make a few phone calls. I'll be in the office for a little while." Raynee said as she grabbed a bowl of soup and glass of water.

"I'm going to run some errands. If you can stay until 6:00, then I'll close up tonight."

"Deal. I am exhausted. But take tomorrow off, I'll be here all day." She held up her hand as Sara began to protest. "Seriously, I mean it. Just enjoy the day."

"If you're sure. Thanks." She grabbed her purse and keys. "See you in a few hours then."

Raynee picked up the spoon to take a bite of the soup, then pushed the bowl away. She didn't have an appetite. She was definitely not a stress eater. In fact, she was the opposite, when things were bothering her, her appetite plummeted.

She dreaded placing the call to check on Payton. It wasn't because she didn't want to talk to her; it was more concern about the condition she would find her in. She had thrown out all of the alcohol she found, but if Payton wanted it, she would have gotten more. She picked up the handset, then place it back down. She took several deep breaths then dialed the number. Payton answered on the fourth ring.

"Yeah." Her voice was weak and sounded like she had been crying.

"Hi Payton, it's Raynee. I just wanted to check on you. How are you doing today?"

"Okay."

"Have you eaten anything today?"

"I think so," she said sullenly.

"I got you some groceries yesterday. Do you think you can fix yourself something? You really need to eat."

"I was waiting for you."

Raynee wasn't expecting that comment and was hesitant to respond. She didn't want Payton to depend on her, yet she wanted to be supportive. "I'm working today Payton, I won't be able to come over."

"Oh."

Raynee heard the soft sobs. She instantly felt horrible. Thinking quickly about the evening, she calculated the time. She could run by on her way home, but could only stay long enough to make sure Payton ate something.

"Look, Sara's coming back later, I'll come by when she gets back. I won't be able to stay long. Okay?

"Okay. Thanks Rayn. I really appreciate it."

"See you soon then." As she hung up the phone, she began to rethink her plans for the evening. She had planned to cook for Lauren, but she would have to go to the grocery store to pick up a few things. She could get takeout, but that wasn't appealing. Then it hit her, *Duh, you do own a restaurant.* She quickly scanned the menu in her mind then went to the kitchen to place a to-go order.

◊◊◊

Raynee had avoided telling Lauren about her lip when they spoke on the phone. It really wasn't a big deal, but she knew she wouldn't be able to hide it when they saw each other. She decided she preferred to tell her in person.

Lauren was leaning on her car in Raynee's parking garage when she pulled up. Raynee gathered her things as Lauren opened her door to greet her. As soon as Raynee looked up, Lauren gasped.

"Baby, what happened to your lip?" She reached out, placed her hand on Raynee's chin and turned her face from side to side examining the swollen lip.

"It's nothing. Let's get these things inside and I'll tell you about it." She handed the insulated bag containing their dinner to Lauren as she exited the car.

Once they were settled inside and had emptied their hands, Lauren pulled Raynee into her arms. She kissed her nimbly on the side of her face and pulled her in for a hug. "I missed you so much. It seems like ages since I last saw you." She spoke affectionately into her ear as they embraced. Pulling back, she looked Raynee in the eyes. "Now tell me what happened to those beautiful lips."

"Would you like a glass of wine? We can talk before we eat." She extracted herself as she selected a bottle of wine from the chiller.

"Sure."

They each collected their glasses of wine and settled on either end of the couch. Taking a sip, Lauren commented on the wine. "This is really good. You're turning me into a wine lover." Setting the glass on the table, she leaned forward and took Raynee's free hand. Looking her in the eyes, she said, "What happened sweetie? You seem to be a little apprehensive in telling me. But you can tell me anything. Now, is there someone I need to go take care of?"

She laughed as she said it, but Raynee knew she was very serious. "Let me start at the beginning." After reminding Lauren about not having her phone at the beach, she told the story of Payton's aunt dying and her going over to check on her. She explained that Payton had a nightmare and when she tried to wake her, Payton has accidentally hit her lip with her elbow.

Lauren listed attentively as Raynee replayed the details of the previous day. She tried to keep her facial expressions neutral and her emotions in check. She was concerned that Payton seemed to rely so heavily on Raynee. She kept telling herself Payton had just lost the last member of her immediate family and how such a loss might affect her if she were in the same position.

Raynee watched Lauren's face as she spoke. She was concerned Lauren would be upset that she had spent the entire previous day attending to Payton. Their relationship was still new and they were learning about each other. While they were at the beach, she felt they had reached a new level in their relationship. She didn't want this situation with Payton to place any doubts in Lauren's mind about where this might go.

After she finished, she slipped across the couch to Lauren and kissed her delicately on the lips. Raynee flinched at the contact to her swollen lip, but was determined to let Lauren know how she felt.

"So, that's the story." She looked up at Lauren to try to gauge what she was thinking and how she felt about what she had just told her.

"You are a good friend to her. I hope she knows that." Stroking Raynee's arm she continued. "I just hate you got injured in the process of doing a good deed."

"It's really not a big deal."

"It is when it keeps me from being able to kiss you the way I want to." She smiled as she leaned forward and kissed Raynee in the spot of her neck she knew would get a rise out of her.

"Umm...well that didn't hurt. You can kiss me there as much as you want."

◊◊◊

After dinner, they returned to the couch. Lauren sat on one end and Raynee snuggled up beside her. She placed her head on Lauren's shoulder as they chatted and listened to music.

"Are you working Saturday night?" Lauren asked as she suddenly remembered the department party.

As she awaited a response, Lauren realized Raynee had fallen asleep on her shoulder. She reached across to wake her, when Raynee stirred and sat up.

"Did I fall asleep? I'm so sorry."

"It's okay, sweetie. Let's get you to bed. You've had a long week already with so much going on."

"Can you stay the night?" The look on her face was almost irresistible.

Lauren reached over and placed her hand on Raynee's cheek. "I would love to, but you really need to get a good night's sleep and I'm afraid if I am here that won't happen." She kissed Raynee's cheek. "Come on, I will help you get ready for bed and tuck you in before I leave. Is that okay?" Standing, she took Raynee's hand to assist her up.

They embraced and held each other for so long Lauren was afraid she had fallen asleep again. She released her embrace slightly and Raynee pulled away.

"Thank you for being so great. I really dreaded telling you about my lip. Thank you for understanding about Payton."

"I know you care about her, Raynee. She's a part of your life."

"I will always care about her. But she is my past...and you, beautiful lady, are my present and my future." She gently touched her lips to Lauren's. "I love you, Lauren."

Pulling her back into a warm embrace, Lauren spoke tenderly in her ear. "I love you, too."

Reaching down, she took Lauren's hand in hers. "Now it's

time to put this girl to bed."

Hand in hand they walked back to the bedroom, Raynee turning off the music and lights as they made their journey.

Lauren sat on the bed talking to Raynee as she completed her nighttime ritual. When she walked back into the bedroom, Lauren looked up and her mouth fell open. Raynee stood before her in the most beautiful birthday suit she had ever seen.

Raynee reached down and pushed Lauren's jaw closed. "Are you sure I can't talk you into staying the night?" She placed her hands on her hips and wiggled her eyebrows.

Lauren looked down at the bare toes in front of her and took her time traveling up the length of Raynee's body until their eyes met. Slowly she expelled the breath she had been holding. "You drive a hard bargain lady." Standing, she took Raynee's hand and led her to her side of the bed. "Get in here and stay warm. Let me brush my teeth and I'll be right back."

Raynee climbed in and Lauren pulled the cover over her. Leaning down she kissed her gently on the swollen lip. Moaning, she turned and ran to the bathroom.

After Lauren quickly washed her face and brushed her teeth, she walked back into the bedroom. Looking at the bed, she realized Raynee was fast asleep. With the motions of a lion on the prowl, she stealthily crawled in beside her. Lauren snuggled against her back and carefully placed her arm across her waist. A still sleeping Raynee settled into her embrace.

◊◊◊

The sound of a phone ringing woke them very early the next morning. Glancing at the clock, Raynee moaned. "Who in the world is insane enough to call this early?" Jumping up, she sprinted to retrieve the offending object from the kitchen counter. Glancing at the display, her expression went grim.

"Payton." She tried to keep her voice from sounding as irritated as she felt.

A very inebriated Payton obviously tried to form her thoughts, but the words came out a jumbled mess. "Ishyacominoberferbrekfess?"

Raynee's heart fell. How in the world could someone be this drunk and awake at 4:20 in the morning? "Payton, no I cannot come over for breakfast." Sighing, she took a deep breath. "You need to go to sleep."

"Budidcntslepwizoutya. Pleez Ray." She could barely speak through the sobs that erupted through her entire body.

"Payton, I'm sorry, but I have to work today. I can't come over. Please stop drinking and try to get some sleep."

Raynee, standing at the counter naked, was shivering when Lauren walked in carrying her robe. She draped it over Raynee's shoulders and placed her hand on the small of her back rubbing in small circles. She looked at Raynee with concern. She mouthed, "Are you okay?"

Raynee shook her head as tears streamed down her face. "She's drunk," she mouthed.

Lauren reached out her hand to take the phone. Raynee handed it over.

"Payton, this is Lauren. This isn't a good time for Raynee to speak with you. Why don't you take a nap? Perhaps the two of you can speak later when you are sober."

Lauren heard the click on the other end of the line, then placed the phone back on the counter. Turning, she pulled a now sobbing Raynee into her arms.

"Come on, let's go lay down." She took Raynee's hand and

guided her back to the bedroom. Once she had her settled back in the bed, she scooted in beside her and took her hand. "Do you want to talk about it?"

Raynee's tears had dried for the most part. She sniffed and shook her head. "I don't even know what to say. I'm so sorry she woke us up...and in that condition. I don't know what she is thinking."

"I know she is going through a rough time right now, but I don't like her upsetting you like this." Lauren was not only worried about Raynee, she was angry with Payton. She bit her tongue in an attempt to control her anger. "Do you want me to speak to her?"

Raynee squeezed Lauren's hand. "No, sweetie. but thank you for being so chivalrous." She turned, wrapping her arms around Lauren and burying her head in her chest. "Just hold me, please."

Lauren slid down in the bed and adjusted so she could wrap her arm around Raynee and held her until they both fell back asleep.

A few hours later they both woke to a much gentler music channel on the alarm clock. They both stirred and stretched, then turned to face each other. Lauren reached over and pushed the hair off Raynee's face. "Good morning, beautiful. How are you feeling?"

Raynee took Lauren's hand and rubbed her palm over her face. "Your skin is so soft. I love your touch." She placed a kiss on Lauren's palm, then looked in her eyes. "Thank you for taking care of me this morning. I'm okay. Just worried about Payton. I just don't know how to help her. Before, I would have talked to her Aunt Janice. Now, I just don't know."

"Honey, it's not your job to fix her. She has to do that herself. Perhaps you should suggest she talk to someone. What about her medical doctor, to begin with?"

"I know, you're right. She has to quit masking the pain with alcohol. I'll talk to her. Maybe I can convince her to talk to Dr. Rogers." She stroked Lauren's hand and she thought about talking with Payton. It was not a conversation she was looking forward to having. She didn't want any more early morning wake-up calls, so perhaps she should expedite the conversation. Maybe she could go by to see her after the lunch rush this afternoon. Giving Lauren's hand a squeeze she added, "Thank you. I'll talk to her this afternoon."

CHAPTER 24

The stadium was almost filled to capacity. Raynee, Lauren, Chandler, and Alex had arrived early enough to secure seats affording them optimal viewing. There was electricity in the air. Perhaps it was just the sheer fact this part of the students' lives was coming to an end, or perhaps it was because Christmas was in a few weeks. Either way, the stadium was abuzz with activity. Suddenly, the organ could be heard throughout the stadium and the crowd immediately became quiet. Raynee could feel the chill bumps break out on her arms, like they did every time she heard *Pomp and Circumstance* played. She shivered involuntarily and Lauren wrapped her arm around her and pulled her close.

All eyes were peeled as they waited for Sam and Lexie. Even though they would be at the end of the group as they marched into the auditorium in alphabetical order, Raynee moved to the edge of her seat with her hands grasped tightly under her chin.

Chandler nudged Alex with her elbow. When Alex looked her way, she pointed toward Raynee. "She is one proud sister," she whispered in Alex's ear.

Alex looked at Chandler who was grinning from ear to ear. She couldn't help but smile too. "She's not the only one. You look just as excited as she does."

Shrugging her shoulders, she tried not to look embarrassed. "Sammie's like a little brother to me."

"I know honey, we are all so proud of him and Lexie." She leaned over and placed a kiss on Chandler's cheek. "It's exciting to see him and Lexie begin the next chapter of their lives."

After what seemed like hours of speeches, they finally witnessed Lexie, then a few minutes later, Sam, cross the stage and accept their diplomas. Even though they had been asked by the president of the university to hold their applause, the foursome couldn't help but stand up and clap as they crossed the stage. The disapproving stares from those around them didn't go unnoticed, but they didn't care. They were so elated they didn't even try to contain their enthusiasm.

After Sam arrived back in his seat, he sent a text to Raynee. "Thanks guys. You trying to get me kicked out of my own graduation?"

Raynee passed her cell phone down for everyone to read the message. They all laughed as they read, once again earning disapproving looks from those around them.

As soon as the ceremony was over, they headed to Pabulum where Raynee had a special dinner planned for the graduates.

CHAPTER 25

It took several conversations over the past few months and a lot of convincing, but Payton had finally agreed to talk with her psychiatrist. Dr. Thomas was meeting with her five days a week and Payton seemed to be making progress. Christmas was in a few days and Dr. Thomas was concerned about Payton being alone. She had encouraged her to spend time with friends and not stay at home by herself.

Raynee spoke to Payton once or twice a week, but was purposefully trying to keep her distance. She knew Payton was extremely vulnerable now and she didn't want her getting the wrong idea about her concern. Payton held a special place in her heart and always would, but her life was with Lauren now, and she didn't want to blur the lines for Payton as to what their relationship was now and would be in the future. On the other hand, she didn't talk about Lauren and their relationship because she didn't want to feel like she was throwing it in Payton's face. It was a fine line, and she was trying to be very careful about how she handled it.

Chandler and Alex were hosting a Christmas Eve party at their home this year. It was something they had done in the past and really enjoyed. Raynee knew how Chandler felt about

Payton, but she had approached her about including her this year. Chandler was more receptive to the idea than she thought she would be. Her friend had a big heart, although she tried to be tough.

A few days before Christmas, Raynee called Payton for her bi-weekly check-in. "Hi Payton, how are you doing?" When she called, she never knew what to expect; although over the past week she had noticed a subtle difference in her mood.

"Hi Rayn. It's a pretty good day today. I actually met with some potential clients about selling their home."

"That's great. I'm glad you are beginning to work a little." It was a nice relief to see Payton starting to take her life back and not rely on a bottle to get her through the day.

"I'm working from home some. I can't go back to the office yet. It's just too hard. I'm thinking about selling the building and either moving to another location or just working out of my guest house." Payton had a small guest house that she rarely used, located behind her main house. It was a perfect setup for her to use as a realty office. It would get her out of the main house, allowing her a place to work without daily facing the place where Aunt Janice died.

"I think that's a really good idea Payton. The guest house would be perfect. You primarily meet the clients at their home or you are out showing them potential homes, so that would work nicely." She paused, considering her words before she continued. "What did Dr. Thomas say about it?" A few times when they had talked, Payton had been very reluctant to share what she and her doctor discussed. She wasn't trying to find out what they talked about, she just wanted to make sure Payton was consulting with her before making any major decisions.

"She thought it was a good idea too. She is encouraging me to get out of the house and start to socialize more."

"How do you feel about that?"

"I think I'm ready."

"Great, then how about you come to our Christmas Eve party? It's going to be at Alex and Chandler's house this year."

"I don't know Rayn, you know Chandler and I aren't the best of friends."

"I already talked to both of them. They would love to have you. Besides, it's time to put the past behind us and bury the hatchet." She softened her tone before adding, "Please..."

"Are you sure? I mean...I don't know..."

"I'm positive. It will be a lot of fun. You don't have to stay long if you aren't having fun or if you feel uncomfortable."

Payton thought for a few minutes before she answered.

"Are you still there?" Raynee wondered if the call had been disconnected.

"Okay, I'll come."

"Great. That's great Payton." she smiled, genuinely pleased Payton had accepted the invitation.

"What can I bring?"

"Nothing, we have everything covered. Just come over anytime after 7:00. You've got the address, right?"

"Yep. I guess I'll see you Friday night then. Thanks, Rayn. Goodnight."

"You are welcome. Night." Raynee disconnected the call and sat back in her desk chair. She was very pleased to hear the change in Payton. She seemed much better tonight. She thought back about the Payton she had found just a few weeks ago. For one thing, she was sober, but she also seemed optimistic about her future and that made Raynee happy.

The knock on the door brought her back to the present. One of the servers stuck his head in the door. "The Williamsons are here celebrating their fortieth wedding anniversary. I thought you would want to know."

"Absolutely, thanks for letting me know." She jumped up and headed out to congratulate the regulars on their special day. On her way past the bar, she grabbed a bottle of their favorite wine.

◊◊◊

"How did it get here so fast?" Chandler was running around putting the finishing touches on the table. It was 6:20 and the guests would be arriving soon. She made a slow 360 degree turn as she evaluated each area within her sight. Mentally, she checked off her list as she turned. Music playing- check. Christmas tree lights on - check. Front porch and outdoor lights on - check. Candles lit - check. Burners in warming trays lit - check. Fresh flowers on the tables - check. She turned back to the table filled with crab cakes with remoulade, shrimp platter, grilled vegetable kabobs with her latest marinade, miniature crab martinis, smoked chicken bites, miniature bacon macaroni, and cheese cupcakes...the list went on. Everything looked to be in place. She walked back to the kitchen and scanned the desserts: chocolate and butterscotch fondues with a variety of fruits and cookies for dipping, miniature kahlua cheesecakes (the only thing Sam had requested) and assorted petit fours she had spent the last two days making. She smiled as she walked to the bar just off the dining room. Alex was behind the bar and had just completed going over everything with Kim, the bartender they had hired for the night.

Alex walked from behind the bar with two glasses in her hand. She handed one to Chandler and then held hers up to give a toast.

Chandler accepted the glass and looked up at her wife with a questioning look.

She touched her glass to Chandler's and looked into her eyes. "To you and tonight. Everything is beautiful, baby. I just wanted to thank you for all of your hard work. I know how much you enjoy this, but I also know how much our friends enjoy it. I appreciate all of the time and special touches you put into making this a perfect evening. So, this toast is to you, the love of my life. I love you and am so happy to be your wife."

Both ladies took a sip from their respective glasses and smiled at each other.

"She outdid herself again. Raynee should open a wine shop. She definitely knows her grapes."

"Don't tell her that, she'll probably try to do it. You two need to get your cooking school going before she starts another business."

"That's true. I'm just glad we can always count on her to provide the wine when we have dinner parties." Reaching out, she took Alex's hand. "Let's go get me changed." Looking over her shoulder, she winked at Kim. "You are in charge until we get back. And don't come looking for us if you don't see us for a few hours."

Kim laughed as she watched the couple walk away. *One day I hope to have a relationship like those two.*

◊◊◊

Alex assisted Chandler in changing and they walked back into the living room as they heard the front door open. Raynee and Lauren walked in hand in hand.

"Wow ladies, it looks great in here," Raynee exclaimed as she perused the room.

"Yes, and it smells divine," Lauren said as she approached the table with her hand extended.

"Hey, what are you doing?" Chandler spoke more harshly than she intended.

"Just making sure it tastes as good as it looks." She stuck the crab cake in her mouth. "Oh my, this is delicious."

Chandler smacked her on the hand. "Now stay away until the other guests arrive." She scolded as she tried to hide her smile.

"But I'm just trying to help. Besides, I missed lunch today so I'm starving."

"Then go to the kitchen and get something from the backup trays."

Lauren quickly turned toward the kitchen, not waiting for Chandler to change her mind. She came back in a few minutes with a small plate filled with various bite-size snacks.

"Poor baby." Raynee handed her a glass of wine then snagged one of the snacks and popped it in her mouth.

"Watch it...a hungry woman is a dangerous woman." She turned her body slightly, putting the plate between herself and Raynee.

"Now girls, there is plenty to eat. Don't fight," Alex snickered at her cousin. Seeing the two of them together made her heart full. She never thought of them as compatible, but seeing them together, she knew it was a perfect match. They were both incredible women and complimented each other perfectly.

The doorbell rang announcing the arrival of the first guests. Over the next half hour or so, the guests arrived and everyone began mingling, eating, and drinking. It turned out to be a beautiful evening; so many of the guests migrated to the deck where Alex had built a fire in the stone fire pit.

Lauren happened to be close to the front door when the doorbell rang once again. She looked up to see Alex in a conversation. She held out her hand to indicate Alex to stay where she was as went to open the door.

When she opened the door, Payton stood before her. "Hi Payton, come on in."

When she realized who Lauren was she looked very surprised. "Oh...um...hi," she finally stuttered.

"Let me take your coat." She held out her hands to assist, but Payton quickly pulled back.

"It's okay. I can get it." Payton looked around the room, avoiding Lauren's eyes.

"Sure, you can just hang it in the closet here." She indicated the closet to the left. "There are plenty of hangers." Lauren stepped back, allowing her space.

Payton hung her coat, then turned and surveyed the room as though she were looking for someone in particular.

Lauren watched Payton and her obvious discomfort. Knowing Payton didn't spot Raynee right away, and wanting to ease her anxiety, she stated, "Raynee was on the deck a few minutes ago. Why don't you go out and let her know you arrived?"

"Yeah, okay." She turned and headed to the back deck like she couldn't wait to get out of the space she shared with Lauren.

As she passed the bar, Payton made a quick stop. "Hi, a bourbon neat please."

Kim poured the drink and handed it to the guest along with a napkin.

Payton threw back the drink in one shot and placed the empty glass back on the bar. "One more please."

Kim looked up, evaluating the attractive woman before her. "Sure thing." She wasn't here to monitor the drinking, but she did feel obligated to make sure no one drank too much and put themselves or others at risk. She would have to keep an eye on this one. As she handed over the drink she indicated the table full of platters of food. "Make sure you try some of the food. Chandler really outdid herself this time."

Payton glanced at the food as she headed to the deck. Downing the drink in her hand, she placed the empty glass on the table as she walked past.

◊◊◊

Raynee was standing at the rail talking with a friend from culinary school and her husband when she felt an arm wrap around her and a warm kiss on her cheek. She turned to introduce Lauren to her friends, only it wasn't Lauren. Payton stood beside her with a huge smile on her face.

"Hi, baby. You look stunning." She took in Raynee from head to toe, the look on her face like she was undressing her.

"Payton, hi. I didn't know you had arrived." Raynee was embarrassed by the obvious attention. Turning to her friends, she made quick introductions. The smell of alcohol on Payton's breath didn't escape her notice.

Turning back to her friends. "It was good to see you both. Let's get together soon." She quickly took Payton by the elbow and guided her towards the house.

"Where are you taking me baby?" Payton wiggled her eyebrows as a huge smiled crossed her face.

"To get something to eat."

"I'm not really hungry. Let's get a drink instead." She put her arm around Raynee, placing her hand dangerously close to her breast.

Raynee gently turned out of the unwanted embrace. "I'm hungry, go with me to get a bite. Chandler has quite a spread. It looks fantastic." She turned, heading for the table.

"Okay, you get food, I'll go get us a drink. What would you like?" She took a step away then turned back when Raynee didn't answer right away. "What do you want Rayn? Wine?"

"I'll go with you." Raynee was not happy to accompany her to the bar, but felt she might be able to get her to drink some water. *Ha, who was she kidding?*

As they approached the bar, Kim looked up and smiled then looked over at Payton. "You're back, do you want the same?"

"Yep, and keep'em coming." Payton stumbled a little, and grabbed the edge of the bar to stable herself.

"What are you drinking Payton?" Raynee inquired.

"Bourbon, neat."

Kim started to pour the bourbon when a slight motion from Raynee caught her attention. Raynee had taken a step back, so she was slightly behind and to the side of Payton. She held up both hand like she was pouring from two bottles and mouthed, "Mix it."

Kim caught on immediately and turned so Payton couldn't see her add water to the drink. Smiling, she handed the glass to Payton. Turning her attention to Raynee, "What would you like Raynee?"

"Water with a twist of lime please." As she stepped up to accept the drink, she silently thanked Kim. Then whispered, "Keep an eye on her and let me know if you have any problems, please."

Kim winked and whispered back, "You got it."

When Raynee turned back to Payton, she noticed she had already drunk half of the bourbon. Taking Payton by the elbow, she led her to the dining room. She picked up a plate, extending it to Payton.

"I already told you I'm not hungry." Holding up the glass, she took another large drink. "This is hitting the spot."

Several minutes later, Lauren approached, stopping at Raynee's left side. "What did you guys find good to eat? Everything looks so delicious."

Payton glared at Lauren, turned, and walked back outside.

Raynee looked at Lauren and said apologetically, "I'm sorry baby, she smelled of alcohol when she arrived. I was trying to get her to eat, but she only seems interesting in getting hammered. I really wish she hadn't come at all. But she sounded so much better when I talked to her a couple of days ago. I don't know what happened."

Lauren pulled Raynee into her arms. "She isn't your responsibility."

"I know, but I just worry about her. She just went through a terrible loss. It isn't easy losing a mother, or in this case, a mother figure."

Gently rubbing her back, she spoke quietly in her ear, so others wouldn't hear her. "But she's an adult and she knows the alcohol isn't going to bring her aunt back. She needs to find another way of coping with her loss."

Pulling back from the embrace that felt so good, she looked into Lauren's eyes. "I know, but I also know how it feels to lose someone so important in your life," she stated heedfully.

She leaned over and placed a kiss on Raynee's lips, then pulled back looked into her eyes. She placed her hand on her cheek. "I wish I could have been there for you when you and Sam lost your parents. I can't imagine how hard it must have been."

"It was, but let's focus on tonight - it's our first Christmas Eve together and I want to have a good time."

"The first of many. Now come on, we can't let all of this yummy food go to waste." She handed Raynee a plate and took one for herself. They walked around the table filling their plates.

They found an empty spot in the den and sat to enjoy their hors d'oeuvres. Alex joined them for a few minutes, snagging a few bites from Lauren's plate.

"Thanks, I'm starving."

"Hey, hey, there's plenty in case you didn't notice. Quit taking mine."

"I just wanted a bite. I've been so busy socializing I haven't had time to get anything." She reached over and took another shrimp, popping it into her mouth. "Um...I married well." She laughed as she walked away.

A few minutes later Chandler rounded the corner, "There you are. I've been looking all over for you. Did you know Payton is here and she is drinking like a fish?" She was obviously irritated.

"Yes, I saw her earlier and tried to get her to eat something, but she wanted no part of it," she said, feeling guilty because she had practically talked Chandler in agreeing to invite Payton. "I'm sorry."

"She's not your responsibility, Raynee. I just don't want her embarrassing herself."

"If she is still drinking like she was earlier, then she can't drive."

"She hung her coat in the hall closet, perhaps she left her keys in the pocket. I can check." Lauren added.

"You check her coat pocket, and if they aren't there, I'll see if I can get them from her," Raynee said. But she dreaded that conversation if it came to it.

Lauren came back a few minutes later shaking her head. "No dice. She must have them on her."

The look of concern was obvious on Raynee's face. She shook her head and said, "Guess I should go ahead and get this over with before she gets worse."

"I'll go with you," Lauren said.

"Me too," chimed in Chandler.

"Calm down Xena," she chuckled at the two of them, her protectors. "She can get verbally nasty when she drinks too much, but she won't get physical. I'll be fine." She turned to walk to the back patio. Lauren and Chandler both followed close behind her.

When they approached the back door, Raynee turned and placed her hand up to stop her new guards. "Stay here, you can watch from a safe distance. Only come to my aid if she picks me up to body-slam me. I would hate to ruin this new dress." She chuckled and walked out the door.

Lauren and Chandler were watching intently from the French doors. They stood back enough so they could see out, but didn't think they could be seen from outside. They jumped when Alex walked up behind them and placed a hand on both of their shoulders.

"What are you two up to?"

"Geez, you about made me wet my thong," Chandler scolded as she turned to face her wife.

"TMI, Chandler." Lauren burst out laughing, almost spewing her sparkling water in Alex's face.

"We're just helping Raynee."

"Helping her? What does she need help with?" She looked around the patio "Where is she anyway?"

Making a quick 180-degree turn, Chandler and Lauren both leapt for the door and were out before Alex could react.

Quickly searching the patio and not seeing either of them, they agreed to split up and look for the missing duo. Lauren walked into the back yard, past the lights of the patio. Chandler headed around the house towards the front yard.

As Chandler rounded the front corner of the house, she ran into Raynee. Startling each other, they both yelped.

Chandler was the first to respond. "Hey, we lost you for a few minutes, where did you go?" Looking around, she continued. "Where's Payton?" She looked back to Raynee and realized she was crying. She took her by the shoulders and pulled her so she was looking into Chandler's face. "Are you okay? Did she hurt you, 'cause if she did I will--"

"No, no, I'm not hurt. She got mad at me and she left. I tried to get her keys, but she was adamant she was okay to drive. I tried to stop her, I really did, but she took off running and jumped in her car before I could stop her." She laid her head on Chandler's shoulder and cried.

Lauren turned the corner and heard Raynee crying. "Where is she?" She spun around, searching for the source of her partner's pain.

"Shh...she's okay. She's just upset. Payton took off before she could get her keys."

"So she's driving? What an idiot. Doesn't she realize when people are trying to help her?" Lauren was furious not only because Payton had driven herself, but at how much she had upset Raynee. She placed her hand on Raynee's back, rubbing soft circles. "I'm sorry honey. I just hate it when she upsets you."

Raynee pulled back from Chandler's embrace. "Thanks Chan." She turned to Lauren. "I'm okay, sweetheart. I just feel her pain and want to help her, but I know I can't. I need to leave that to the professionals. I just hope she makes it home safely and doesn't hurt anyone."

"We all do, Raynee," Chandler said as she turned them all back to the house.

CHAPTER 26

Payton jumped in her car and locked the doors as she saw Raynee looking up and down the street for her. No way was she taking her keys and leaving her stranded. She had tried to get Raynee to leave all of this and come away with her. Just the two of them. She loved Raynee...didn't Raynee realize it? But Raynee didn't return her love, not anymore. Not since Lauren had come to town. Why did she have to come here and screw everything up for her? She could have had Raynee back and they could have been happy.

Payton pressed the accelerator and she fishtailed away from the curb. She had to get away from here...this party, these people, and especially Raynee. She was furious with herself for losing her again. She just couldn't get it together where Raynee was concerned. She loved her so much, but every time she was close to getting her back, she did something stupid and screwed it up. Now she had no one. She lost her mom, her aunt, and Raynee...she had no one and she would never find anyone to love her, not the way Raynee had. At the beginning, it was so good with them, then those nightmares started happening again. She just couldn't cope and she let the painkillers destroy her relationship with Raynee. Now she had done it again...

The curve snuck up on her; she was so engrossed in her thoughts of Raynee she didn't see it in time. She stomped on the brakes, but it was too late. The tree was there in front of her and then everything went black.

◊◊◊

Payton heard the sirens but couldn't open her eyes. The pain in her head was excruciating. Suddenly, she felt someone touching her shoulder. She screamed at the unexpected contact.

"Miss, are you okay? Try to calm down. We are here to help you. Can you hear me?" The voice was consoling. "We're going to get you out of here, Miss. Just stay calm. Can you tell me if you hurt anywhere?"

"Getyastinkinghandsoffame, letmeouttahere," she slurred. Turning to open the door, she realized she was pinned in.

"Just try to relax. I'm Joe and I'm a paramedic. You have some cuts on your head. It looks like you hit the steering wheel pretty hard. Can you move your arms okay?"

"Getmedahellouttahere...NOW!" she screamed.

"Tell me your name. I want to help you."

"Ion'tneedyourdamnhep. Getmeouttahere."

"Ma'am have you been drinking?" Joe kept talking to her and was trying his best to calm her, but the more he talked the more belligerent she became.

"Dat'snoneofyourbiznes. GETMEOUTTAHERENOW!" she screamed at the top of her lungs.

"Hi, Joe." David spoke as he approached with the Jaws of Life.

"Better get the captain over here," he spoke tolerantly, "She's had more than a few. She's getting pretty agitated."

David turned his back to the car and spoke into his collar microphone. "Captain - we've got a 10-55 over here. You may want to have a couple of guys on standby for when we get her out. She's not very cooperative."

◊◊◊

Payton woke up with a splitting headache. She raised her hand to her head and felt the dried blood. Sitting up on the bed, she looked around. She was alone in a small cell. She swung her legs to the floor, put her elbows on her legs, and leaned over to place her hands in her head.

She remembered someone poking and prodding her. She vaguely remembered the doctor sewing up the cut on her face. She reached back up and felt the bandage on her forehead. "Damn." She removed her hand and shook her head to try to clear more of the cobwebs.

Why am I in jail? Then it hit her. She remembered drinking a lot at the party...well, okay and a few before she arrived at the party. She remembered talking to Raynee and trying to get her to leave with her. "Oh shit." She remembered seeing the tree heading straight for her...or rather she was heading straight for it. She lay back down on the bed. *What have I done?*

Payton looked up as the officer approached. "You're awake. Good. Is there anyone you want to call?"

"Just someone to get me out of here."

After calling the bondsman, Payton went back to her cell and fell asleep.

The rain was coming down so hard she could hardly see the road. Then everything went dark. Before her eyes adjusted to the blackness, a bright light started coming straight toward her. The lights were so bright. She reached to pull down the sun visor. But the lights kept heading straight for her. She jerked the wheel of the car. The next thing she heard was....

The sound of the cell door opening woke her. She turned toward the door and opened her eyes. She reached up and wiped the sweat from her face as she sat up.

"Your bond has been posted. You can go now, ma'am. The officer up front will give you your paperwork and your personal effects. If you need a ride, he can call someone for you."

Payton was so embarrassed she didn't know what to say. She stood and walked towards the open door.

"You be careful now ma'am. You could have hurt yourself worse than you did or you could have hurt someone else. I know it's the holidays and all, but just be careful."

Payton looked up at the young officer, nodded her head and walked out.

There was no way she was calling anyone to come to get her. Who would she call anyway? She had no family; she couldn't and wouldn't call Raynee who was her only friend. Well, *was* is probably the right word, she thought. Who knew if Raynee would ever speak to her again. She walked into the sunshine and got into the waiting cab. After giving the driver her address, she leaned back in the seat and shut her eyes. Her life was officially a mess. She had totaled her car, lost her only friend, and now she would have a DUI on her record. Things couldn't get any worse. *Merry Christmas Payton.*

CHAPTER 27

Lauren woke to the smell of coffee. She stretched across the width of the bed but found it empty. She opened her eyes to see a very naked woman standing at the foot of the bed - two steaming cups in her hands. She knew one was coffee, the other herbal tea.

"I woke up and you weren't here." Lauren sat up, exposing her naked body, a pout on her face.

"I was standing right here watching you wake up my love." Raynee set the cups on the nightstand, and sat on the edge of the bed.

"I missed you." Lauren looked at her with a frown on her face.

"You didn't even know I was gone." Raynee chuckled and shook her head.

"I still missed you...when I was sleeping." Brushing her hand across Raynee's cheek. "I miss seeing this beautiful face." Leaning toward her, she continued. "I miss these lips." She kissed the softest lips she had ever felt. Reaching up, she touched Raynee's breast. "I miss these girls too." She placed a kiss on each, lingering on the nipple before raising her head to look back into the green and brown eyes looking back at her with admiration. She loved Raynee's eyes - so unique - so beautiful - so full of life. "Merry Christmas, beautiful."

"Merry Christmas, my love. I hope you slept well."

"I did, when you finally let me go to sleep. You bad girl." She winked.

"I was just trying to keep you up so we could see if Santa came." Raynee feigned innocence.

"Uh hum...good thing Santa didn't walk in here...boy would he have been surprised." She laughed out loud.

"Are you ready to see if he came after you went to sleep, or would you like breakfast first?"

"Well, I am famished. You wore me out last night, or should I say this morning. Think we could eat a quick bite then check for evidence of the big guy?"

"How about I heat some of the cinnamon bread I made and we can eat while we investigate?"

"Think we should put some clothes on first?"

"Well, we did already initiate my couch, but yes, let's put something on." Raynee opened the dresser drawer, grabbing a couple pairs of pajamas. "We don't want you catching a cold...or anyone seeing this gorgeous body through the windows." She tossed one pair to Lauren.

They quickly threw on their pajamas - neither sure why they even had pajamas since they never slept in them.

Raynee headed to the living area while Lauren went to the bathroom. She hurriedly flipped a couple of switches then went to the kitchen to cut the bread and preheat the oven.

Raynee looked up when Lauren walked into the living area to find a lit Christmas tree overrun with multi-colored packages underneath. The fireplace was crackling, and she could hear ever so lightly the sound of Christmas music playing through the speakers mounted in the ceiling throughout the kitchen and living area.

"Oh Raynee, it's beautiful. Thank you, honey." Rushing to the kitchen, she spun Raynee around and pulled her into a tight embrace. "I am the luckiest girl ever. I love you so much."

"No, I'm luckier. I am so happy you came into my life and we are sharing our year of firsts." She placed her lips on Lauren's and tried to convey the emotion overflowing in her heart.

◊◊◊

Mid-afternoon, Sam and Lexie arrived with gifts in tow. They were catching up and enjoying mimosas when Chandler and Alex arrived.

As they settled onto the opposing couch with drinks in hand, Chandler asked, "How does it feel to be out of school? Are you guys excited and ready to join the working class?"

Sam and Lexie exchanged looks, smiling at each other. "I'm ready. How about you honey?"

"I may as well be, nothing I can do about it now. I am glad to be out of school, that's for sure." Lexie added. "Seven years of college is enough for me."

"How long before you take your bar exam?" Lauren inquired.

"I'm going to start working right away at the firm with Alex while I study. I'm shooting for March first." Sam looked over at Lexie then added, "Lexie's going to try to take hers at the same time. We both want those past us before the wedding."

"You guys have a lot going on. I don't envy you at all," Chandler said.

Lexie looked at Sam, a huge smile crossing her face. "It will all be worth it to be able to spend the rest of my life with this man."

A collective "Ah" filled the room.

"Anybody hungry?" Raynee inquired.

Before she could finish asking Sam was up and heading for the kitchen, calling back over his shoulder. "I am!"

Everyone was laughing as they all joined Sam at the dining table for their annual Christmas day meal.

Raynee looked around the table at this group - her family by blood and by choice. She was so thankful for each of them. Sam and Lexie would be married in a few months. Eventually she hoped to be an aunt. It would be nice to have a little niece or nephew around the table. She had never wanted any of her own, but it would be nice to have nieces and nephews to enjoy, spoil, and then send home. She chuckled aloud. Raynee looked up to see everyone looking at her.

"Something you care to share with the rest of us?" Chandler teased.

"Not really," she replied with a huge smile on her face, but she was blushing slightly.

Lauren reached over and placed her hand on Raynee's leg. "Are you okay sweetie?"

"Yes, I was just thinking about how our family is growing. It makes me very happy." She placed her hand on top of Lauren's.

The chit-chat around the table continued without a hitch, discussing everything from the wedding, the plans for the cooking camp, and the party the previous evening.

Raynee hoped to avoid the part about Payton, but everyone here was also at the party and knew what had transpired.

"Have you heard from her?" Sam looked at Raynee.

"No," she replied bluntly.

"Are you going to call her?"

"I don't know. I'm really upset with her." Raynee really wanted this conversation to end. She looked up at Sam and gave him *that look*. He took the hint and changed the subject.

CHAPTER 28

The day after Christmas, Payton walked out of Dr. Thomas's office an emotional wreck. She had called the doctor to make an emergency appointment. She felt like she was falling apart and needed to try to get some clarity. During her session, they talked a lot about the dreams - especially the new ones she had been having the last few months. She understood the dreams of herself as a young child, but she couldn't understand the new dreams where she was an adult. Today's session had changed all of that. She sat in her car in the parking lot replaying the parts of the dreams she remembered. There had to be a way for her to get to the bottom of this. They had to mean something, but the fragmented pieces were beginning to come together and she didn't like how the puzzle looked. She wished she could control the dreams, when they happened and how much she remembered. Dreams...ha, who was she kidding, call them what they really were: nightmares.

She cranked the rental car she had picked up this morning and stopped by the liquor store on the way home. At least she could drink there in peace and not have to worry about hurting anyone or some stranger telling her when she had enough.

As soon as she walked in the door, she went directly to the

kitchen, poured herself a hefty glass of bourbon and downed it. She poured another and took it with her to the bedroom where she changed into a pair of lounging pants and a T-shirt.

After she got comfortable, she sat down with a notepad and pen...and, of course, another glass of bourbon. She was going to take Dr. Thomas's advice and write down everything she remembered about the nightmares. If she kept doing this every time she had a new one, perhaps she could figure out what they meant. She hoped with all her heart it didn't mean what she thought it did.

CHAPTER 29

With the holidays behind them, Chandler and Raynee began searching in earnest for the perfect venue for their new venture. Alex recommended Jane, a friend she had worked with who was a realtor. They had met several times and looked at a few places, but nothing felt right.

Since the debacle with Payton before Christmas, Raynee didn't feel comfortable working with her. In fact, she had distanced herself from Payton entirely. Payton was on a self destruction path once again and Raynee knew she had to step aside. She had tried many times for many years to help Payton. She now realized not only was it not her job, Payton wasn't her responsibility anymore. She still loved Payton, but she had to save herself. When they were in a relationship, she felt responsible and did everything she could to try to help Payton deal with the trauma of her childhood. If Payton wanted to go down that path, Raynee couldn't be part of it this time.

Raynee was in her office at Pabulum preparing the menu specials for the day when her cell phone rang. Looking down and recognizing the number, she quickly answered the call.

"Hi Jane. How's it going?"

Her voice bubbling with excitement. "Please tell me you can spare some time for me today. I think I found the perfect place for you and Chandler."

Jane had the perfect personality for her profession. She had such a warm inviting demeanor. She listened carefully to what her clients said and didn't waste their time by showing them places that were unrealistic or didn't fit their needs. Her energy seemed to be contagious. No matter what else was going on, when Jane was in the room, you suddenly felt happy.

Raynee smiled at the enthusiasm spilling through the phone. "I'll have to check with Chandler, but I have some time later, say around 2:00?"

"I'll call Chandler and see if she can meet us at 2:00. I'll call you right back if it doesn't work for her."

"Can you give me any clues about what you found?" Raynee inquired, curious about the recent find.

"It has great outdoor space, plenty of grown potential, outside the city, but not too far." Jane continued. "I really think you are going to love it. Trust me on this one. Meet me at my office and I'll drive."

"Okay then, I'll see you in a few hours unless I hear back from you after you speak with Chandler."

"I can't wait," Jane chuckled. "Bye."

Raynee hung up and smiled at the phone. Jane was an awesome find. Too bad she didn't have a girlfriend. She would be a great partner for the right lady. *Hum, who do I know I can set her up with?*

◊◊◊

Raynee pulled into Halley Realty a few minutes past 2 p.m.

As she approached the door, Chandler and Jane met her as they walked out. Jane handed her one of the bottles of water she was carrying.

"Let's go ladies."

"Shotgun!" Chandler shouted as they headed to Jane's car.

Raynee and Jane laughed at Chandler's antics.

"That girl will never grow up." Raynee laughed.

"What's the point in growing up?" Chandler questioned.

They pulled out of the parking lot of headed northeast. As Jane drove, she provided more details about where they were going and what to expect.

"This property just came on the market today. It's about twelve acres. Partially wooded, but already has four buildings, which are in really good shape."

"Wait a minute...twelve acres? Jane, we want a small space, not a farm." Chandler turned in the seat as she spoke. She looked back at Raynee who sat behind Jane.

"I know it's more than you were thinking about, but just hear me out."

"I agree with Chan..that's a lot more than we had in mind." Trying to keep an open mind, she turned to Chandler. "Let's hear her out, Chan."

Chandler nodded her head. "Go ahead then, but I don't know about this."

"I understand, but wait until you see it. It's about ten miles out, which wouldn't be too far for a client to travel and not far for you guys either. But it's isolated, so you have privacy. They have a fence around the perimeter, so you wouldn't have that expense."

Chandler turned and looked at Raynee. Raynee read her expression and smiled, "It sounds nice. Let's take a look before we totally discount it."

Jane slowed the car and turned left. She approached a gate about 25 feet from the road. Reaching down, she grabbed a remote from the cup holder. Aiming the remote toward the gate, she pressed the button and the large gate slowly began to open.

"Now that's pretty sweet," Chandler exclaimed as she turned to face Raynee. Both of them had huge smiles on their faces.

They traveled down the tree-lined drive for about a quarter of a mile before they came to an opening. There was a large gravel parking lot on the left. To the right was a large covered pavilion. To the left past the parking lot was a smaller building resembling an office. Past the smaller building, in the distance were two additional buildings.

Chandler and Raynee were both out of the car before Jane put it in park. The ladies were pointing and chatting when Jane joined them, smiling in a knowing kind of way. She was pleased at their obvious excitement. "Where should we start?"

"The pavilion!" Chandler exclaimed.

"The office!" Raynee shouted at the same time.

The trio laughed in unison. "Let's start at the pavilion. I have some ideas I want to share."

As they surveyed the pavilion, Chandler and Raynee started discussing how they could set up the classroom and the cooking area. They were both excited when Jane showed them the large storage room running the length of the building, which would be perfect for housing the supplies. They continued their tour of the office, which had a full bath and two rooms that could be used as bedrooms.

"I know this wasn't part of your plan, but let's take a look at the other two buildings." As they walked to toward the structures, Jane asked, "What do you think of the place so far?"

Chandler indicated to Raynee, who proceeded, "My mind is going ninety miles an hour. This really wasn't what I had in mind, but I see so much potential here." Turning back to Chandler, "What do you think Chan?"

"I agree, it's much more than we were looking for, but I love that it's away from the city, but not too far. I love, love, love the pavilion. We could do so much there with classes. It has great storage. It's quiet out here. The buildings are in great shape."

Jane unlocked the door to the first building and they stepped into a large room with a fireplace on the far back wall. The room was the size of a large living area. There were hallways on both sides, which led to two smaller rooms on each side. Each room had a private bathroom. Jane explained the other building was identical to this one.

"This is nice Jane, but we wouldn't need all this space. And the way it's laid out, we couldn't sell this part," Chandler thought aloud as they continued the tour.

"I don't think you would want to. What if you held onsite camps for adults? You could charge more to cover the expenses and adults would love a getaway place yet still be close to the city."

"I like the way you think, Jane. We hadn't talked about overnight guests. But we could hold multi-day classes or even an entire weekend, Chan."

"Or maybe do a couple of classes during the week. If we have housing available, it does open the potential for a variety of classes. Family classes, classes for kids, or adults only."

"But, we haven't even discussed the price yet. I think this place is way over our budget," Raynee interjected.

"Yea, there's that too," Chandler agreed.

"Let's sit down and look at the numbers. Then the two of you can do come crunching to see what you think. I think it has a lot of potential, it's in great shape and the location is great."

"I agree with you on all of those points. I'm open to the idea of overnight guests, but it's something we need to discuss." Raynee looked to Chandler.

Chandler nodded her agreement. "I love the space. Really, what's not to love?" Placing her arm around Raynee as they walked back to the car, "We have a lot more to think about now my friend."

◊◊◊

After Jane drove them back to her office, they sat at her conference table and discussed the price of the property. The ladies agreed to let her know within the next day or two if they wanted to make an offer on the place.

As they walked to their cars, Raynee suggested they get together later to talk about the camp. "Why don't you and Alex come over around 6, I'll throw something on the grill? Lauren is coming over, so Alex will have someone to talk with if they get bored listening to us."

"Sounds great," Chandler said as she got in her car and pulled away.

Raynee cranked her car and immediately begin thinking of

the possibilities presented to them today with the camp property. She smiled as she sang along with the radio. She knew she and Chandler were both seriously considering the property. Her mind began racing with ideas...she hurried home to begin getting them on paper.

◊◊◊

Raynee was sitting at the dining table, paper spread out and her laptop powered on. She had the layout of the camp Jane had provided and had begun making lists on her laptop. Based on the numbers Jane had provided, she was able to calculate roughly what their monthly payments would be. Then she started a list of possible camps they could hold. Obviously, classes for different skill levels, varying by age groups and specialty classes. She and Chandler would both agree they would like classes on grilling, desserts, even a basic introduction to cooking class. She was deep in thought when she heard the front door open.

"Hi, baby." She turned as Lauren walked through the door. "I'm glad you're home."

Lauren smiled at the reference to this being her home. "Hi sweetheart. How was your day?" Perusing the contents of the table, she approached. "What are you up to?"

Raynee beamed as she went over the events of the day. She knew as she was telling Lauren, she had already made up her mind about the property. She just hoped Chandler agreed.

"That sounds like a great place, honey. What does Chandler think?"

"She and Alex will be here..." She looked up at the clock, "in about an hour to talk about it and hopefully make a decision." Raynee beamed.

Lauren pulled her in for a hug, "It sounds like someone

already decided."

"I think I have, but this is definitely a joint decision." Raynee confirmed optimistically.

CHAPTER 30

Payton's body jerked as she screamed aloud. The shrill cry woke her as she thrashed around on the bed. She sat up with a start and realized she was covered in sweat. The sheets were wet, her chest was wet. She reached up and ruffled her hair, which was also soaked. She shook her head as the pieces of the nightmare played back through her mind.

It was her first year as a licensed realtor. Memorial Day weekend she had clients in town who were in a hurry to find a place, so she had worked all weekend with them. She knew she still had so much to learn, but they were a pain. She was trying her best to find exactly what they wanted. Today had been extremely difficult. After showing the newlyweds a dozen houses, she needed and deserved a drink. She had gone to her favorite hangout and stayed longer than she thought she would. Beth, the bartender, had cut her off. She offered to call a taxi and as she turned to make the call, Payton slipped out the door and headed to her car.

It was a moonless night and a light cool rain fell gently from the sky. By the time she reached her car in the back of the parking lot, the droplets fell from her hair into her face. The streets glistened in the streetlights from the rain settling on the asphalt. It was a short drive to her new house, which was one reason she had chosen to go to the Sports Page tonight. She drove south on Piedmont, the rain coming down harder now. Only a few more blocks to Cheshire Bridge Road. Focus Payton, she kept telling herself. She wiped the rain from her eyes. All of a sudden, the streetlights went black. The sudden projection into blackness startled her. She blinked several times, trying to adjust to the charcoal surrounding her as the downpour pummeled her car.

She looked to the left, her street should be right here. Did she miss her turn? As she turned back, she was blinded by the bright headlights that suddenly appeared and were heading straight for her. Jerking her wheel to the left, then realizing she was heading straight for the lights, she tried to correct. That's when she felt the impact. She jerked the wheel again and thrust the gas pedal to the floor. She could hear the screams as her car careened past the bridge that crossed over Peachtree Creek.

That was it, she realized as she felt the tears flowing down her face. Finally the missing pieces. She shivered as her damp skin began to dry. Jumping up, she grabbed the abandoned T-shirt and sweat pants from the chair and ran down the hall to her office. She pulled on the clothing and sank into the chair. She opened the web browser and pulled up the website she was looking for and held her breath as she began to read.

◊◊◊

Payton sat staring at the monitor.

Atlanta Journal Constitution - September 2 - Award Winning Local Chef William Waters and Wife Elaine killed in hit-and-run accident.

Her hands were shaking. *It can't be ...it just can't be.* She screamed aloud to no one. *God, I need a drink.* She jumped up and ran for the kitchen, almost tripping over the chair in her haste. She grabbed the bottle of scotch sitting on the counter, unscrewed the cap and turned the bottle up to her lips. She took a large swallow, and then a second before placing the bottle back on the counter. She wiped her mouth with the back of her hand. The tears were still flowing down her cheeks. She clutched her chest. The stabbing pain was unlike anything she had ever felt. She thought for a few seconds she might be having a heart attack. *How could she ever fix what she had done? How did this happen? How could she ever fix this?* But she knew the reality; she would never be able to do anything to fix what she had done. She grabbed the bottle and slid down the wall until she hit the floor. Between screams and tears, she emptied the bottle and fell over when she finally passed out.

CHAPTER 31

Chandler and Raynee sat with Jane at the conference table in her office. Stacks of papers were splayed in front of them.

"Are we ready to do this?" Jane inquired searching the faces of both ladies.

Chandler and Raynee both smiling from ear to ear looked at each other than to Jane. Together they replied, "Let's do it!"

Jane reviewed the contract before them and explained about the inspections she recommended they make part of the contract. After reviewing the numbers once more, she handed each of them a blue pen. "Okay ladies, once you sign, I'll call their realtor and make the offer. Hopefully we won't have to wait long to hear back from them."

Taking pens in hand, they both signed the offer and slid is across the table to Jane.

"Do you want to wait here while I make the call?" Jane inquired as she rose to go back to her office.

Looking to Chandler for her confirmation, Raynee replied, "Sure, then we'll go grab a bite to eat. Would you like to join us?"

"Just give me a couple of minutes to call this in and check with my assistant. I'll be right back."

After making the call, Jane came back to the conference room.

"I need to do a little more paperwork for another client. I can join you in about a half hour. Is that okay? At Pabulum?"

Rising and pushing her chair back under the table, Chandler answered, "We will be easy to spot. We'll be the two poor ladies at the bar."

◊◊◊

About an hour later Chandler and Raynee were sitting in the bar area at Pabulum. It was close to 2 p.m., so the lunch crowd had thinned out. They were sharing an appetizer and chatting with Sara as she stood behind the bar.

"There you are," Jane exclaimed as she approached. Both turned on their barstools to face their new realtor. "Congratulations ladies."

"What do you mean?" Chandler inquired.

"Did they accept our offer?" They spoke at the same time.

"Yes, they did. Congratulations ladies, you are now the proud owners of Camp Chow."

Raynee and Chandler jumped up and pulled each other in for a hug. Not to be left out, Sara ran around the bar and threw her arms around her friends. Pulling back, they motioned for Jane to join them in the group hug.

"Oh my gosh, Raynee, what have we done?" Chandler beamed as she looked up at her friend.

"I think we have started the next phase of our careers my friend," Raynee declared.

"This deserves a toast. I am so happy for you both. Although things aren't going to be the same with you gone Raynee. I'll miss you, but I really am happy for both of you."

Everyone cheered as Sara opened the bottle of Champagne to celebrate the occasion.

CHAPTER 32

Payton woke face-down on the floor. She felt stiff from lying on the hard floor. Slowly, she sat up and looked out the window. It was dark outside. She strained to see the time on the oven clock, but her vision was still blurry. She climbed to her feet. The pain in her head now matched what she felt in her heart. She clutched her chest, the pain echoing throughout her body.

She walked into the den and sat in the dark on the couch. Sinking into the leather, she placed her arms on her knees and her head in her hands. Random thoughts ran through her pounding head. *The newlyweds, the bar, the scotch, the storm, the darkness, the bright lights, the sounds of screams and the loud crash.*

Pulling herself up, she walked back to the kitchen and took a drink from the bottle on the counter. She stood there for several minutes, staring into space. She knew there was only one thing left to do. Grabbing her cell phone and car keys, she headed out the door.

◊◊◊

Raynee and Lauren were lying on the couch watching a

movie. It had been an emotional day and Raynee needed to relax and watch something that didn't require any thought. The latest Sandra Bullock movie was doing the trick. They were both laughing at the antics of the actress when the phone rang. Raynee grabbed the phone from the end table as Lauren pressed pause on the remote.

"Hello," she answered. She heard breathing. "Hello, is anyone there?" She heard the click as the phone disconnected.

Placing the phone back on the cradle, she turned back to Lauren. Shrugging, she responded to the unasked question. "I don't know. They hung up when I answered."

"Must have been a wrong number. You don't use your landline very much. Why do you still have it? I got rid of mine years ago."

"I really don't know why I keep it. I should cancel it." Jumping up, she announced, "Nature break, then we can finish the movie." Leaning down she placed a kiss on Lauren's forehead, then drew her finger down her cheek. "This has been a great day and an even better evening. I can't imagine being any happier than I am right now. Thank you for coming into my life."

Smiling, Lauren stood and pulled Raynee into her arms. She placed kisses around the perimeter of her face then on the sides of her neck. "Me too, sweetie. You fill the hole in my heart that has been there for so long. I love you...always remember."

◊◊◊

Payton pressed the end call button on her steering wheel. She had left her house in such a hurry she didn't bother to think where Raynee might be. Luckily, she was home. She didn't want to tell her over the phone and didn't even want to alert her she was on her way to her house. She didn't want to take a chance of Raynee not allowing her to come over. She would just show up - that was the best way. There was no easy way to tell Raynee what she had to say.

Payton's mind wandered as she thought about what she would say. She replayed different scenarios, but nothing sounded right to her own ears. How could she ever make Raynee understand? She had to find a way to make her understand it was an accident. She never meant to hurt anyone. It was just an accident.

She shook her head, trying to clear it. The taste of scotch was still strong in her mouth. She reached down and grabbed the bottle of water from the cup holder. She didn't care that it had been in her car for a couple of days. She unscrewed the cap and poured the warm liquid down her parched throat.

The sound of screeching tires drew her attention forward, then as if in slow motion, she turned to the left as the car careened into her driver's side door. The metal pierced her body and the shards of glass covered her as the impact pushed her car into the opposing traffic, sandwiching her between the cars. The last thing she heard was her own screams as her world went permanently black.

EPILOGUE

Raynee pushed her feet into the warm sand. Her hands splayed behind her, she closed her eyes and turned her face upward drinking in the warmth of the sun. The tears ran down her face as she slowly opened her eyes looking towards the clouds. So much had changed in her life over the past several months. Jumping up, she wiped at her face and turned to jog back home.

She plopped down on the end of the chaise and placed her hand on Lauren's bent leg. "Hi, baby. I missed you."

Lauren lowered the book she was reading and pulled off her sunglasses. Leaning forward, she placed a kiss on Raynee's lips. "Did you have a nice run my love?" She looked closer into Raynee's eyes and saw they were red. She dropped the book on the patio as she turned and pulled Raynee into her arms. "Oh, honey, what's going on in the beautiful head? Do you want to talk about it?"

"I'm sorry - it just hits me sometimes." Her voice cracked and tears spilled over her cheeks as she spoke. "My parents died way too young. You know today would have been their fortieth anniversary. So many lives cut short for no apparent reason."

"I know you miss your parents and Payton. They were very important influences on making you who you are today." She kissed Raynee on the top of her head as she held her close. "I wish I could take away your pain."

Raynee wiped the tears from her eyes. "I'll never understand how three people who were so important in my life died at the hands of irresponsible drivers." Pulling back, she looked up at Lauren with a forced smile. "I better get it together, we have a big day ahead of us."

"I know they are all looking down at you now and are so proud of you and what you have accomplished. Could you have imagined six months ago your first month of classes at Camp would be sold out? Raynee, you are an amazing woman. I am so happy you chose me to share your life. I am the luckiest girl alive."

"I'm glad we have each other. We are going to have a wonderful life together."

Standing, she reached out her hand.

Lauren placed her hand in Raynee's and stood, pulling her close. "I love you...always remember," she whispered as she hugged her close.

Pulling back, they sealed it with a kiss. Then placing their arms around each other, they walked into the house to wake Sam. He had lots to do - it was his wedding day.

The End

ABOUT THE AUTHOR

Denise Judge knew for many years she had a story inside just waiting to come out, but life kept getting in the way. Twenty years later she is proud to hold her first novel, ALWAYS REMEMBER, in her hands. A southern girl at heart, she and her partner now live "up north" in Richmond, Virginia.

www.ingramcontent.com/pod-product-compliance
Lightning Source LLC
Chambersburg PA
CBHW070103260626
47160CB00004B/1300